WISHBONES

and other

Short Stories

MARY FLYNN

Author site: www.MaryFlynnWrites.com

Cover art by Michael Butler
Michael by Design, Graphic Design Services,
www.TorqueCreativeLLC.com

ISBN 978-1-7328380-4-8

Dedication

For My Mother

"The more I know about God, I am convinced He likes to read books and authors are His librarians. Every soul is a story waiting to be read."

— Shannon L. Alder

OTHER BOOKS BY MARY FLYNN

— • —

— FICTION —

Margaret Ferry

— POETRY —

As One Deligted

— NON-FICTION —

Disney's "Secret Sauce"

The Little-Known Factor Behind
The Business Wordl's Most Legendary Leadership

— CHILDREN'S —

Reggie & Rocky

The Ring-tailed Raccoons

Reggie & Rocky

The Naughty Raccoons

— MIDDLE GRADE —

Mrs. Peppel's Pillows

Other Published Works

— • —

The Saturday Evening Post Anthology of
Great American Short Fiction

14th Annual Writer's Digest

Short Short Story Competition Collection

CONTENTS

ACKNOWLEDGEMENTS

I would like to acknowledge the writers who made a great impression on me as I read through my library's entire short story section when I was in my thirties—O'Henry, Ring Lardner, John Cheever, Shirley Jackson, Carson McCuller, Isaac Bashevis Singer, Mark Twain, John O'Hara, William Faulkner, John Steinbeck, Anton Chekov, Joseph Conrad, Edith Wharton, Katherine Anne Porter, Flannery O'Connor and James Thurber. I acknowledge with gratitude the many friends who encouraged me along the way, as well as the Sisters of St. Joseph at St. John the Evangelist in Brooklyn who valued good reading and writing skills nearly above all others. And, of course, my wonderful mother who read to me every night when I was a child and later allowed me to make my very first trip on my own to the public library many blocks from home.

Shatanja, Devil Cat

THE ONLY CAT I ever owned crept into the clothes dryer one day and ended up going a little cuckoo from half an hour of tumbling amid the hot towels. She was never the same.

I wasn't quite the same either, having to deal with the poor cat who now walked sideways across the floor, her coal black hair standing on end as if in a perpetual state of electric shock. One side of her mouth was permanently turned up and her right eye rolled about or looked off in a different direction from the other.

Shatanja was a stray I had taken in. A friend of mine who once lived in Istanbul came up with the name, Shatanja, Turkish for devil, and she really looked the part following the tumble-dry incident.

The vet, amazed but not worried, checked her over and brought her fever down. "She'll be a bit quirky," he said, "but she'll live. That's one tough cat you've got there."

Before long, Shatanja was back to her old habits, perched on top of the refrigerator to bat the head of anyone walking past. But it didn't work out for her quite the way it used to—her depth of field had been compromised by that one unreliable eye, and she no longer had the ability to land on her feet, as cats famously do. This was never more evident than the day Mrs. Ortega stopped by to pick up some tablecloths for the bake sale.

It was a chilly fall day and Mrs. Ortega came in wearing a knitted scarf around the collar of her coat. As the stout little woman walked across the kitchen, Shatanja whacked at the top of her head several times, but missed due to the woman's short stature and Shatanja's impaired vision. Mrs. Ortega was completely unaware of this until Shatanja lost her footing and fell off the refrigerator onto the back of Mrs. Ortega's head.

Mrs. Ortega screamed. I panicked and Shatanja panicked too—apparently aware that having neither claws nor the ability to right herself, she was on her way to the floor, headfirst.

As Mrs. Ortega flailed about to free herself of her feline attacker, I tried frantically to get a grip on Shatanja, but she had already grabbed hold of Mrs. Ortega's knitted scarf with her teeth. The terrified woman twisted wildly to shake off the cat, but the scarf only grew tighter under the weight of Shatanja's descent, pulling Mrs. Ortega backwards. The cat squealed and so did Mrs. Ortega.

Just as I managed to loosen Mrs. Ortega's scarf, Mrs. Cannon appeared. Mrs. Cannon, who had been waiting outside in the car for Mrs. Ortega, heard the terrible commotion and came rushing in. She took one look at the horrifying spectacle of an animal being hurled about on her friend's back, grabbed a pan of dishwater from the sink and threw the water onto Shatanja, dousing me and Mrs. Ortega, as well.

How could Mrs. Cannon have known that I had been soaking an empty pickle jar in the dishwater to remove the label? The pickle jar flew from the pan of water and knocked Mrs. Ortega out cold.

Before the EMT's arrived, I managed to drag Shatanja down the hall by Mrs. Ortega's scarf and fling her (the cat, not Mrs. Ortega) into the far bedroom.

Mrs. Ortega turned out to be all right and I tried to return her scarf. I even bought her a new one, along with her favorite coconut cake, but neither she nor Mrs. Cannon ever spoke to me again.

"Who would be crazy enough," they'd been heard to grumble, "to keep a devil cat as a pet?"

I wish I could say that Shatanja learned her lesson, or that I found a far-away ranch willing to provide a happy dwelling for weird little creatures such as "devil cats," but I can't. Shatanja learned nothing from the incident. And neither did I? Still, I couldn't turn her away. Yes, she had been given fair warning about the dryer and, yes, she had disobeyed. But I often wondered how my own life would have turned out if I had suffered the full consequences of my misdeeds. I was lucky. Poor Shatanja was not. And things did not improve.

Like Cato, the karate-maddened valet to *The Pink Panther's* Inspector Clouseau, Shatanja jumped out from everywhere and nowhere, often with very unpleasant results, the worst of this occurring on the day I made a blueberry trifle for the ladies' club gatherimg. Perhaps you can imagine where this is going. If so, you are correct. On the one hand, I was relieved that Shatanja had made herself scarce during the preparation and cooking. But anytime Shatanja remained out of sight for very long, I had a certain uneasiness.

As I carried the large glass bowl full of trifle across the living room, headed for the front door, Shatanja leapt from the top of the china cabinet onto the dining room table then flew past my head like a low-flying bat.

I ducked in time, but was thrown off balance. Unfortunately, the trifle was thrown off balance, as well. The great glass bowl did not leave my grip, but as if in slow motion, it rotated just enough to part company with the trifle.

In a matter of moments, blueberry slog came pouring over me like magma, and cascaded to the carpet. From the corner of my eye, I saw Shatanja lick her paw, then sidle off down the hall. At that moment, I actually considered putting her back in the dryer.

Three weeks later on Halloween night, Shatanja had a redemption of sorts. I was at the movies when two neighborhood boys broke in through the dining room window to rob the place.

I can only imagine what happened when the young thieves took their first step into the dimly lighted room and saw a black cat walking sideways toward them, hair standing on end, one side of its mouth curled up, one eye rolling uncontrollably in its head. What I do know is that they ran screaming from the house and never stole again. It was rumored that one of them later went into the seminary.

After that, fewer and fewer people came to visit, especially those who remembered Mrs. Ortega being carried out on a gurney, soaked to the skin, with a knot on her head the size of a cue ball. Mine, after all, was the house of "the devil cat," and I was in some regards "the devil cat lady." I considered moving, but in an odd way I had come to relish the mystique.

Over the years, I was invited more than once to bring Shatanja to a Halloween event of one kind or another, but couldn't bear the thought of making a spectacle of her. We had somehow managed to get along and I was at her side when, at the age of nineteen, her electrified hair finally settled itself and she closed that one crazy eye to go to her final peace.

The Prayer

ONE MORNING ALISON came out of her room happy as could be. No moping around. No doom and gloom. She looked like her old self again. The change startled me.

"What happened to you?" I asked, as I watched her move about the kitchen, more animated than she had been since that one miserable night we were never to speak of again.

"I don't know where to begin, Megan. The most amazing thing has happened."

I wondered what amazing thing could have happened between 10:30 at night and 6:00 the next morning. I had seen her the night before, as I had most nights these past two months, slugging toward her room, waif-like in her oversized plaid flannel bathrobe, belt trailing behind on the floor.

"You won't believe this," she said, shaking her head as she poured her coffee.

"Well, tell me."

"I was saying my prayers. Just lying there. And all of a sudden, a thought came to me. I won't say it was the voice of

God. I don't think anyone actually hears the voice of God, but the thought that went through my head was, 'Ask St. Michael the Archangel for help.' And I said to myself, *whoa, where did that come from?* I had never thought of praying to St. Michael. He's such a big angel. You just don't ask him for stuff like you do St. Anthony or St. Francis. But as soon as I thought it, it seemed right. It felt very…I don't know…strong. So, I asked him to help me with…you know…the whole David thing."

I did know. The whole David thing, as my sister called it, had very nearly sapped the life out of her. That beautiful, vibrant spirit of hers had taken a blow when David broke it off. They had dated for nearly two years. Then one night they went to dinner, and it was over.

Aside from a couple of polite emails telling her how great she was, that it wasn't anything she had done, and how he would always treasure their friendship, Alison had not heard from him again. She didn't believe him, of course, positive that she had done something, perhaps everything, wrong. Where exactly had she failed? The thought never seemed to leave her.

I had suggested we take a trip to get away, go to Paris maybe. She'd always had a love affair with Paris, though she had never been there. But she wouldn't hear of it, which was probably just as well, since neither of us could really afford it.

"I kept thinking how odd," she went on, "odd but powerful. I guess I dozed off about eleven. Then I got up around three to go to the bathroom. I don't know what made me check email. I never do at that hour, but I did, and there was an email from

David. Can you imagine? After two months without a word, there he was. Doesn't that seem amazing to you, Megan…I mean, right after praying to St. Michael for help?"

"What did David say?" I was not a fan.

"Well, it's unbelievable, but he's coming tonight. At 7:00. He's coming back, and St. Michael did it."

My heart sank. "When you say coming back, do you mean…are you…?"

"It means what coming back means, Megan." There was impatience in her voice.

"Well, did he say he wants to get back together?"

"He didn't have to. You forget – we went together for two years. I know how he thinks."

I hardly thought so, considering how stunned she was when he broke up with her.

"Isn't it incredible?" She was childlike, in awe of the moment. I was not. To me, David had always seemed self-absorbed and manipulative.

"Incredible, yes," I said, wondering why an angel would put such a shallow man back into Alison's life.

"And see," she said, mindlessly over-stirring her coffee, and with more than a bit of cockiness in her tone, "if St. Michael is on my side, then it must prove that you've always been wrong about David."

"Well," I said, reaching for the cream, "St. Michael must know something I don't." I recalled the David who forgot important dates, the David who criticized Alison in front of others.

She bristled. "Maybe he knows about that beautiful and expensive diamond pendant David gave me our first Christmas together."

Alison never cared about expensive things, but the pendant was extraordinary – a glistening black onyx oval, with an inner edge of seed pearls, an outer edge of diamond baguettes and a stunning pink diamond at the center – a most generous expression of his rare kindness. But that was earlier in their relationship and he did seem crazy about her at first. Many months would pass before even Alison began to notice his true nature.

The doorbell rang at seven sharp, quite unusual, I thought, for the man who had never once been on time. Alison sprang from her room, long auburn waves flying, exuberant in her white pullover, tight jeans and four-inch black patent heels. The pendant hung around her neck, weighty on its gold rope chain. Regardless of what I thought about David, I was happy for the occasion to see my beautiful younger sister full of spirit again.

I had promised to make myself scarce and headed out of the apartment as David headed in. We exchanged quick but polite greetings. He looked well. He'd always had a kind of GQ look about him, with a salon glisten to his thick black hair. Tonight, he carried a larger-than-life bouquet of red roses laced with white baby's breath. Something's up, I thought.

As the door closed behind me with a solid thud, I heard

him tell Alison how awesome she looked. I felt sick at the thought that they might get back together. David was someone I just didn't trust.

I drove across town to see an action thriller too long and too wild for a work night, but I needed the noise to keep from thinking about what might be going on back home.

The movie ended about eleven. Traffic was light. Just the same, I took the long way home. It would be a late night for Alison, as well, but I knew she wouldn't care. I made a lot of noise putting the key in the lock, and fumbled with the doorknob to announce myself. I needn't have worried.

Alison sat alone on the sofa, shoes off, one leg tucked under her. It sounded like the coffee grinder was running. I did a quick scan of the room and saw the bottle of wine she had set out still unopened on the sofa table, the two long-stem glasses unused. It took me a moment longer to figure out what the noise was – as I drew nearer to her, I saw that she was feeding the roses, one by one, into the paper shredder. She stopped when I came around.

"Are you okay?" I whispered.

She nodded. Her eyes were bright. It seemed clear that whatever had happened, my sister had not been crying about it. That alone surprised me.

"Do you want to talk? Can I fix you a cup of tea?"

"That would be very nice." Her voice was soft and surprisingly pleasant for someone whose evening clearly had not gone at all well.

I watched her from the galley kitchen, as I put two cups of water into the microwave. When the tea was ready, I brought it on a tray and sat beside her on the sofa. At first, neither of us said a word.

"Mm. Is this the new African red tea?" she said at last.

I wondered why she seemed so okay with things.

"Yes. I picked it up yesterday at Gristedes. You like it?"

"I love it," she said.

"I do too." My curiosity was in high gear.

Alison took a deep breath without looking up. She held the warm mug between her hands, as if to summon calm from the fragrant steam.

"David is starting up a new company." Her tone was matter-of-fact. "He and his partner will be operating on a shoestring for a while. He needs to raise money any way he can. He asked if I would give him back the pendant so he can sell it."

"What?" This was over the top even for David.

"He said he'd make it up to me when the business took off."

As I fought to contain my anger, I realized Alison was no longer wearing the pendant. If David had still been there, I would have slugged him.

"In a hundred years," she said, "I never would have dreamed of asking someone to give back a gift I had given them. I couldn't have imagined selling a gift someone had given me."

I shook my head. "I'm so sorry, Alison. I'm sorry about tonight. About everything. I'm sorry about the whole...you know...St. Michael thing too."

She set her cup down. "St. Michael did just fine, Megan," she said softly. "He did exactly what I asked him to do. I prayed for help, and that's what he gave me." She looked up. "I finally… *finally*…see David for what he is. I guess it had to take an Archangel to open my eyes." She gestured with her hands, as if receiving a blessing. "Believe it or not, I actually feel free, free of sadness." She looked into my eyes with a resolve I had not seen before. "Free of David."

Her words lifted my heart. "Well, then, I'm just sorry that it cost you such heartache, to say nothing of your beautiful pendant."

"What do you mean?"

"Your pendant. You gave it to him, didn't you?"

"Are you crazy?" Alison laughed. It had been a long time since I'd heard such gusto in her voice. She reached down into one of her shoes that lay on the floor and pulled out the onyx and diamond oval.

I breathed a sigh of relief. "Oh, Alison," I said, and hugged her. "I'm so proud of you. So happy to have you back. And so glad to be rid of…"

"Now, now," she scolded, her tone almost musical. "We mustn't be too hard on David. He gave me something very special tonight…besides my freedom, I mean."

"Not the roses. You've done a number on those."

"Better." She winked, and I saw that old twinkle in her eye. "He gave me a big idea when he said he was going to sell the pendant." She dangled the glittering, precious object in front of me. "We're going to Paris, Kiddo."

Venom

"'Jumpy.' I hate when they call me that, like I'm a rabbit or something. A grasshopper." Leo tossed the get-well card to the foot of the bed. "One of Sanzoni's guys, always looking to jab you. He needs to show some respect. They must think they got me now. I have news for them."

"It's just an old nickname, Boss. They're idiots. You know what the doc said. You gotta take it easy." Manny knew the nickname might be old, long before Leo "Jumpy" Campaneri rose to power in the rackets. But to this day, The Boss was always on edge about one thing or another. Even as a kid, nervous, worried, making things bigger and more fearful in his mind, a trait that followed him into manhood. Everybody knew it and that alone made him want to bite people's heads off.

Manny patted Leo on the arm, just above the crook of the elbow where the intravenous had been inserted three days earlier. "You're gonna be okay, Boss. You're gonna be okay. The heart thing was mild. With rest, Leo Campaneri will be good as new. Hey!"

"He said I'm gonna die, didn't he? No secrets, Manny."

"You're crazy. On my mother's grave, nothin' of the sort. And no secrets. You know everything I know. The doctor said take it easy and don't excite yourself. He could release you by the end of the week. You heard him."

Leo looked toward the window. The late afternoon light turned the walls of his hospital room a soft gold. "The day is fading, Manny. Like my life."

"What are you talkin' about? You shouldn't be thinkin' stuff like that. A heart attack does not mean it's the end of anything. You have a big life, Boss. It's not gonna fade away so easy. Believe the doctor."

Manny was concerned. Leo was stubbornly anxious. All their many years together, Manny had witnessed the pacing and tapping. Leo heading up a meeting, shifting in his chair, his leg shaking up and down on the ball of his foot like a motor. The head of The Family turning a pen over and over in his fingers, a natural-born worrier, and Manny knew that's the kind of stress that finally put him in the hospital.

Leo lay back and stared up at the ceiling. "Sanzoni's waiting now. Circling like a buzzard. The rat. Thinks he'll just walk in and take over everything I spent my life building up." He reached over and, with a weakened grip, took hold of Manny's arm. "Promise me, Manny…"

"I don't want to hear talk like that, Boss. Nothin's gonna…"

There was a light tap on the door and Doctor Lipman walked in with a clipboard and a cheerful hello.

Manny blessed himself. "Boy, Doc, you couldn't have come at a better time."

The doctor smiled. "What's going on? I figured I might be walking in on a poker game."

Leo Campaneri, his thick gray hair flattened on one side, pulled himself higher against his pillow. "You gotta level with me, Doc. How bad is it really?"

"Well, I'd say not bad at all." The doctor glanced at a couple of the clipboard pages. "The sun's been out all day, the temperature about 74. And it looks like it's going to be a clear evening with lots of stars. Pretty good, huh?"

Manny eyed Doctor Lipman then turned to Leo, unaccustomed to this kind of reaction to The Boss, and said nothing.

Leo's eyes narrowed. "Is this something to joke about, Doc?"

"I guess what I'm suggesting, Mr. Campaneri, is that you consider more joking and less worrying. We talked yesterday. I tried to assure you that you'll be fine with rest and relaxation. I have to wonder just what it's going to take to convince you you'll be fine. Your situation is not unusual. Your blood work looks good, and the equipment doesn't lie." He gestured to the monitors. "The readings have been steady and uneventful. Your blood pressure is reasonably under control. The new medication will help with that." He patted Leo on the shoulder. "Relax, Mr. Campaneri. Why not have a game of cards or watch a nice TV comedy? It can do you a world of good."

Leo put his head down and nodded. "I guess you got me, Doc."

Manny took a deep breath and walked to the door with Doctor Lipman. "Thanks, Doc. I appreciate it. We all do." Then he turned to Leo. "What I tell ya? No secrets. You're gonna be fine. I'm goin' out in the hall and see what the boys are doin'. Guido and Artie should be comin' on soon. Hospital Security's been good about them packin'. They understand it's a protection thing for you. They're all good people, Leo. Now, please get some rest."

Leo dropped back against the pillow. "Give the boys my regards." He wished he could find the doctor's words comforting. But doctors lie, he knew that. They lie to your face. It's part of their training. They get your family to lie, and your friends. How could anyone ever be sure?

His thoughts went to Nico Sanzoni. "Waiting to move in, you punk?" He spit the words out as if his nemesis were actually there. "But if the doc is right, you'll wait until you rot, and I'll gloat over your corpse." He knew he had no choice but to do what Lipman said. He would take it easy and get out of there. Manny was right.

Still…

Leo Campaneri and Nico Sanzoni went back a lot of years with a lot of mistrust, betrayal and pain, grabbing after each other's business, spoiling each other's peace. Leo thought about the last time they'd seen each other. What was it now…four, five years? It was at The Fontainebleau in Miami. Sanzoni had tried to move in on Leo's territory. He had even tried to recruit a few of Leo's boys. Things got messy. They both lost a couple of good men that week. But Leo was too swift. He got over on Sanzoni, put the skids on, and while Sanzoni was still in Miami, took over his entire Jersey Shore operation. Sanzoni went into a rage.

"I'll see you on your deathbed, you fat creep," the fifty-year-old Sanzoni had yelled, the artery in his neck as thick as a finger.

"At least I'll have a bed," Leo had shouted back, an inch from Sanzoni's face. "You'll die in the gutter like the bum that you are."

They had not seen each other since, but it hadn't kept Sanzoni from breathing down Leo's neck, always looking for a way in.

Leo couldn't tell how long he'd been asleep. It was dark outside the window now. One of the nurses must have turned the lamp on when she came in to check on him. The covers had been straightened and he felt comfortable and more relaxed. It was possible that the doctor might be right, he thought—all he had to do was rest.

He saw the door open. Manny peeked in and put his finger to his lips. "I didn't want to wake you," he whispered. "You had a good one—a couple hours."

Leo nodded, his eyes still heavy. "What time is it?"

"It's nearly eight thirty." Manny pulled a chair up to the side of the bed and sat down. "Somebody's here, Boss." He leaned in, still whispering. "He's been here over an hour."

"Who? What's wrong?"

"See, that's what I'm talkin' about—why does something always have to be wrong? Something happened that we never figured on, and I think it could be good."

"What are you talking about?"

"Sanzoni's here."

"Sanzoni! That piece of…"

"Wait. Wait." Manny put his hand on Leo's arm, as Leo tried to push himself up. "Take it easy. You know how we always say everything happens for a reason. That's why I think this could be good. Sanzoni's changed, Leo. He's different. He feels bad about what happened. He…"

"Don't believe it, Manny. Don't believe it. He's a snake. No one should know that better than you—what he did to Benny. He's giving you a line."

"Maybe it's time to let all that go, Boss. You scared me this week. I don't want to see you in here ever again. I think Sanzoni sees it too, that this is where we all end up when we carry the hate around with us like poison. It gets in our soul."

Leo had turned away and stared at the wall.

"We checked him, Boss. He's clean. And he's alone. Think about it—nobody's with him, even downstairs. I think this guy's sincere about wanting to square things. Sometimes, things like what happened to you change people's hearts. Sanzoni really feels bad."

"That snake has no heart. He feels nothing, Manny, trust

me."

They sat quiet for a few minutes, with only an occasional truck rumbling over the dark city streets to break the silence.

Manny picked up the green plastic carafe from the side table and poured some water into a plastic cup. He handed it to Leo. "Sanzoni's been eating at your insides for years. It's stuff like that that put you here. Letting this guy apologize to you doesn't make you weak. You're still The Boss. He's not stupid—he got his head handed to him in Miami. He learned. And you've always been fair about givin' people a chance. But this time it's for your own good."

"Sanzoni's had too many chances, Manny." He took a sip of the water, then another sip. "My mouth is like sawdust."

There was another silence

"Let the rat make peace, Leo."

Nico Sanzoni quietly entered the room, flanked by Manny, Guido and Artie. Leo recognized at once the sheen of his signature Hart-Schaffner and Marx custom cut suit and his "lucky" gold cufflinks that gleamed in the lamplight. One ounce of gold short of a pimp, Leo thought.

At the foot of the bed, Sanzoni gave a reverential nod. "You look well, Leo."

"I heard your mother passed away. I'm sorry." Leo put the cup of water on the table. "Why are you here, Nico?"

"What Manny told you is the truth, Leo. Otherwise you would never have agreed to see me. I want to make peace." He looked about at the three men hovering, the bulkiness of their guns visible under their suit jackets. "Can we have some privacy?"

Leo waved Manny to a far corner and motioned for Guido and Artie to leave the room. Then he gestured to the chair near the bed, and Sanzoni sat.

Sanzoni leaned forward, resting his elbows on his knees. "I know you hate me, Leo." His voice was low and calm. "I've hated myself these past years for…you know…for Miami."

"I don't want to get into all that."

"Neither do I, Leo. I want to get past it. Forgive and forget works for so many people. Can't it work this once for us too?"

Leo looked into Nico's face, darkly shadowed as ever even with the impeccably close shave, more lines around the mouth now, black hair, dyed and slick, silver at the temples, and the same musky cologne. The lashes were not so thick as Leo remembered, but the eyes appeared softer. "It's asking a lot, Sanzo."

Nico looked up. "You haven't called me that for over twenty years." He shook his head. "You always knew how to break a heart, Leo."

Leo took a deep breath and shrugged. "We were once kids together on the lower east side. We watched each other's backs. You pulled me out of that alley when I nearly got my teeth kicked in."

Nico smiled. "You know that Testavito kid got the chair ten years later for killing that family in Bridgeport."

Leo nodded.

"And you," Nico said. "You gave me my start, Leo. First, Sheepshead Bay, then Flatbush and half of Brooklyn, on and on. You gave me everything. I didn't deserve your generosity. Now, I need to make it up…while there's still time."

Leo's brain snapped back to reality. He shot Nico a look. "Still time?"

"No. You know what I mean—while you're on the mend, right?" Nico moved in his chair. "They say you'll be out of here in a couple of days. That's all. That's all I meant."

Leo was swept by frenzy. He felt his face flush. *He knows something. He knows something.* His pulse quickened. "The doctors say I'm fine…I just need rest." He rubbed a small fold of the bed sheet between his fingers, and kept rubbing.

"Doctors know best. Right? Right." said Nico. "My mother had a great doctor. And thank you for the beautiful flowers you sent for the funeral. No matter what was between us, Leo, you never lost your class."

"Mrs. Sanzoni was a lovely woman. I would never disrespect her."

"And you'll always be remembered for things like that. Hey, speaking of remembering, you remember, Big Harry? Who ever thought his kid would grow up to be Doctor Villerino. My mother loved him. Well…doctors can't be expected to know everything. And she didn't have much pain at the end. Villerino has what they call a great bedside manner—he was always reassuring her, even when there was nothing more he could do, just to ease her mind. I respected him for that. What'd she have to know, huh? She went in peace."

Leo felt the tightness in his neck, the deepening pressure in his chest. His heart was racing now. He opened his mouth to take in air, the small fold of bed sheet squeezed in his fist.

Nico reacted. "Leo, you're fine. *Trust* me."

The words cut like a razor. What Leo could trust was that Nico Sanzoni would not be here unless The Boss was on his way out. "I'll see you on your deathbed," Sanzoni had said in Miami. Well, here it was. And Lipman was the liar Leo had figured him to be. He could only imagine that Manny and the others were in on it all the time.

The monitors beeped. Fast, then faster. Nico stepped back as Manny hurried across the room to Leo's bedside. An alarm sounded. Leo squirmed, the strain written across his face as he struggled, breathless. He clutched his chest, and let out a low, deep gasp.

Nurses rushed in as a voice on a loud-speaker in the hall announced the *Code Blue.* In a moment, Leo Campaneri's hospital bed was surrounded by medics in pale blue scrubs, working feverishly over their patient.

The tech with the paddles yelled, "Clear," as the monitor flatlined.

Manny threw his hand to his mouth and sobbed.

Guido and Artie stood in the doorway, stunned and speechless, while Nico Sanzoni, unnoticed now, moved easily between them, stealing himself from the frenzy. In the corridor, he straightened his tie and, with a sly grin, made his way to the elevator.

The Cleverest Merchant

IT WAS JUNE in the village of Upper Chenille and that meant one thing—the village council was preparing to select the Cleverest Merchant of the Year. This was a very competitive contest because the prize was $15,000.

The council met in Mayor Toby's office one day at noon. Mayor Toby was not looking forward to the meeting because there was one particular council member who bullied everyone. It was not pleasant.

"You all know why we're here," the Mayor said, then looked directly at Mrs. La Plant. "And, please, let's try to make this year's meeting a bit easier than in the past. Why don't you start things off, Mr. St. William."

The kindly but nervous Mr. St. William moved a little in his chair and cleared his throat. "Well, I've given this a great deal of thought. And in my opinion, the cleverest merchant of the year is Mrs. Laslo." He looked up for reaction. Everyone smiled politely. Everyone, that is, except Mrs. La Plant.

"Surely, you are joking," said the stone-faced woman in

a voice loud enough to blow the wax from an elephant's ear. Everyone jumped.

"Now, now." Mr. St. William went on. "Let me tell you why I feel this way." Again, he cleared his throat and squirmed. "As you know, Mrs. Laslo has doubled the size of her clock store this past year. She has more clocks than any other clock store in all of Pinabree County. It takes a very clever person to make a business grow that much in just one year."

"Hog wash," said Mrs. LaPlant, with a scowl that would frighten the pants off a scarecrow. "She's got more clocks than anyone else because she's not selling any."

"Well, I don't know," Mayor Toby said. "Mr. St. William makes a good point."

"I'm terribly sorry to have to disagree with you," said Miss Ring, in her customary gracious and soft-spoken way, "but my choice for the cleverest merchant of the year is Mr. Wheatley, the florist."

"Wheatley?" they all said at once.

"The Florist," Miss Ring repeated. "Don't you recall that wonderful advertising campaign of his? And that catchy slogan—*Flowers smell sweetly and please you completely when you buy them from Wheatley?*"

Mrs. La Plant shot to her feet. "Oh, that ridiculous slogan. That ridiculous man." She puffed out her chest. "He won't get my vote. You can be sure of that."

"Think what you will," Miss Ring said, "but people went around repeating that slogan for months." She lifted her head, as if with some measure of authority. "Most importantly, everyone in town bought Wheatley's flowers for weddings and club luncheons and school dances, and every other kind of occasion. His name was on everyone's lips. You surely remember that. Only the cleverest of merchants could accomplish such a thing."

"That makes sense," Mayor Toby said.

Mrs. La Plant fixed herself in a rigid pose, head held high, and stared out the window.

The mayor peered over his glasses and glared at her from behind his desk, wishing he had the nerve to throw some heavy object at the back of her head. He took a deep breath and looked to the gentleman sitting to his right. "Why don't you tell us what you've got to say, Mr. Sanchez."

Mr. Sanchez, the council's newest member, stood and faced the group. "I don't have anything against the merchants mentioned here so far. They're very good merchants. I just think that when you all hear what I have to say, you'll agree with me." He tugged at the sleeves of his suit jacket and continued. "You see, I believe that the cleverest merchant in Upper Chenille is none other than Cy Nibner."

"The plumber?" Mrs. La Plant barked. "That's outrageous."

"Mrs. La Plant—please," the mayor said. "Go on, Mr. Sanchez."

"It's easy to see how well Nibner's plumbing store has done this year. He's bought a larger home and a new car and boat. He's even joined the country club. Without a doubt, his

business has prospered. And the remarkable thing is that he has accomplished all of this just by bringing the circus to town."

Mrs. La Plant arched an eyebrow. "A couple of acrobats and an elephant? I would guess, Mr. Sanchez, that only a *clown* would find that clever."

Mr. Sanchez cleared his throat. "Bringing the circus to town did something very important. It made all the children happy. It's a clever merchant, indeed, who knows that by making the children happy, you please their parents. Now, all those parents get their plumbing supplies and services from Nibner. That's what I call clever."

Mr. Sanchez appeared quite pleased with himself. He sat back, arms folded, waiting for the others to agree with him, as he surely must have guessed they would.

"Well, that's worth considering," said Mayor Toby.

"Not in this lifetime." Mrs. LaPlant stepped to the center of the room. "Now that you've all had your say, I'll have mine."

The mayor leaned back in his chair and rolled his eyes.

"Each of you has named your choice," Mrs. LaPlant said, "and I'm not one bit surprised that each of you is completely wrong. It's typical."

What they all knew to be typical was that Mrs. La Plant behaved like a disagreeable bully who always managed to get her way. Most people in town were intimidated by her and some even crossed to the other side of the street when they saw her coming their way. It was all very frustrating, but no one seemed to have the courage to stand up to her. Someone needed to cut her down to size, figuratively speaking, of course.

"Just get on with it, Mrs. La Plant," Mayor Toby said.

Mrs. La Plant threw her head back, indignant. "I shall tell you all that the cleverest merchant in Upper Chenille is Eli Birney."

"Eli Birney?" Even Mayor Toby was surprised.

"That's ridiculous," Mr. Sanchez said. "Birney's shoe store has been on its last leg for years."

"That's quite true," Miss Ring chimed in. "Everyone knows it."

Mr. St. William mopped his forehead with his handkerchief and remained silent.

Mrs. LaPlant appeared undaunted. "Well, despite what you or anyone else may think, Mr. Birney is definitely the cleverest merchant in town. I have watched him carefully, though he doesn't know anyone is on to him. While other merchants were bothering with silly slogans and circus elephants, Eli Birney was quietly making a fortune in his shoe store."

"On what do you base this ridiculous claim?" Mayor Toby asked.

"Very simple. Everyone in town knows I go to Miller's Stationery and Business Supplies Store on Tuesdays to visit Mrs. Miller. And every single Tuesday for the last two months, I have seen Mr. Birney buying bags there. Two hundred bags at a time, to be exact. Mrs. Miller orders them for him special."

"Two hundred bags is an extraordinary number," said Mr. St. William.

"Every week?" Mr. Sanchez wanted to know.

"Every single week," said Mrs. La Plant.

Miss Ring put her finger to her lip and pondered this. "But what does it prove?"

"My good woman," Mrs. La Plant bellowed, "can't you see past the end of your nose? It proves that Mr. Birney has begun selling enough shoes to fill two hundred bags every single week. Do you have any idea how much money that man must be making? And no one even knows how he's doing it."

Again, Miss Ring gave it some thought. "Well, if he's kept it all so quiet, he must be making so much money that he doesn't even care about the competition or the $15,000."

"Precisely," said Mrs. La Plant, slamming her hand on Mayor Toby's desk. "That is cleverness at its best."

The group fell silent. Then they began whispering among themselves. Mayor Toby joined in.

After a few minutes, the mayor said, "Well, it appears we've reached a decision."

Once again, Mrs. La Plant had prevailed.

On the day that Mayor Toby presented the award to Eli Birney, there was great excitement in Upper Chenille. People were astonished at the news that Birney had won, for many had long believed that Birney's shoe store was near bankruptcy. Mrs. La Plant, however, was quick to let everyone know about the bags and about her great powers of deduction. In a way, she had become the real star of the show for having figured it all out. Both newspapers had even run feature stories on her as well as Mr. Birney. The nightly news covered the story for days.

On the day after the prize money was awarded, the council met once again in the mayor's office. This time, they were to discuss the paper drive to support the annual charity fundraiser. Everyone was on time for the meeting except Mr. St. William. This was most unusual, for Mr. St. William prided himself on being as punctual as London's Big Ben. Being late made him much too nervous.

Mrs. La Plant paced the floor. "Oh, where is that man," she snapped. "I don't have all day."

"I can't imagine what's keeping him," said Miss Ring. "I hope nothing has…"

But before she could finish, the door flew open and Mr. St. William came rushing in. He was so out of breath that the others could hardly understand a word he said.

"Are you all right?" Mr. Sanchez asked.

Miss Ring quickly pulled out a chair for him to sit. "Calm down, or you'll have a stroke."

Mr. St. William sat and calmed himself as best he could. "I don't think I'm the one who's going to have the stroke." He looked directly at Mrs. La Plant. "There's something going on over at Birney's Shoe Store. That's what delayed me."

Mayor Toby threw up his hands. "Oh, what now? What now?"

"You'd better come and see for yourselves," said Mr. St. William, still a bit breathless.

"I have no time for such nonsense," Mrs. La Plant said.

"Nor have I," said the mayor.

Mr. St. William went to the window and pointed in the direction of Birney's Shoe Store. "You may not think it's nonsense when you see what's going on over there."

Mayor Toby, Mrs. La Plant and the others left the office and walked over to Birney's Shoe Store. From a block away, they could see the street outside his store filled with people.

"Just what kind of foolishness is this?" Mrs. La Plant demanded to know, totally out of patience. "We should be back at the mayor's office concerning ourselves with the paper drive."

"Well," said Mr. St. William, "if it's the paper drive you're concerned about, this ought to make you very happy."

As they approached, the crowd noticed them and the noise grew louder. The sound of laughter swelled. Whatever was going on certainly amused everyone.

"Look," said Mr. Sanchez, pointing to the yellow panel truck parked along the curb, "there's one of our trucks."

Just then, someone in the crowd yelled. "Hey, Eli, here comes Mrs. La Plant now. Maybe she'll have her picture taken with you again for the newspaper."

The crowd's laughter thundered in the street.

Mayor Toby and the other council members made their way to the front of the store. And there, to their utter amazement, was a grinning Eli Birney, surrounded by stack upon stack of paper bags.

Mrs. La Plant froze still as a statue, her mouth gaping, as the color drained from her face.

Someone from the newspaper hurried over to her. "Isn't it wonderful, Mrs. La Plant? Mr. Birney is getting the paper drive off to a grand start. He's contributing thousands of paper bags. How about I get a picture of the two of you?"

Mrs. La Plant straightened herself and marched over to Birney. "You think this is all very funny, don't you? You horrible dishonest man. You have committed fraud."

Eli Birney gave her a big smile. "I'm sorry to disagree with you, my Dear Henrietta, but all I did was buy a lot of bags. You drew your own conclusions."

Mrs.La Plant wagged a finger in Eli Birney's face. "You knew all along that I go to Miller's on Tuesdays and that I would see you buying those bags. You did all of this on purpose just to try to make a fool of me. You run a failed business. You don't deserve the prize money."

"Ah, but I do," said Mr. Birney. "The award isn't for the most successful business. It's for the cleverest merchant. Now tell me, what is cleverer than winning $15,000 just by purchasing bags? I want to personally thank you."

As the cameras flashed, Mrs. La Plant opened her mouth to protest but, alas, she was speechless.

Not That Sorry

ABBIE TOOK THE paint-soaked roller out of the tray and slapped a swath of café mocha across the wall. "You know he's driving up here just to snoop."

"Hey, don't take it out on the wall, Babe."

"Why did we ever agree to let him come? He doesn't have to drive a hundred and fifty miles just to deliver your check. He's up to something."

David went up behind her and put his hand on her shoulder. "You were right about the color. The contractor's going to be happy we finally decided."

Abbie tilted her head and stepped back to eye her work. "It is pretty, isn't it? But we're not even moved in yet." She gestured to the emptiness of the surrounding rooms. "At least he could have waited a couple weeks. What's wrong with mailing the damn check? That would be the decent thing to do. Oh, wait…I forgot…he doesn't know the meaning of the word."

"All we're going to do is have a bite of lunch with him, Abb, and to tell the truth, I don't mind the chance to show the great

Alton Deaver we can get along just fine without him."

"Maybe it has finally registered with him that Deaver and Associates has lost their best associate, and…oh, by the way… their best creative mind."

David laughed. "He's going to bust when he sees this place."

To Abbie and David, this sprawling house was a dream-come-true—over-sized rooms, a spacious hallway, tall French windows that looked out on an acre of lawn off a street flanked by sycamores, just blocks from the heart of town. It was a pretty amazing contrast to the two-bedroom Riverside Drive condo they'd lived in for the past eight years. Much as they loved New York City, they were ready to give small-town life a try.

Abbie shook her head. "I still can't believe it's ours. Won't it be fun to go back through its history?"

David looked about, nodding. "A hundred years is a long time, but I'll say one thing, this house is still fit as a fortress."

"How could all this have happened in just five short weeks?"

In just five short weeks, following David's resignation from Deaver, they had put their condo on the market, sold it within the week for an amazing price, accepted a long-standing invitation for David to teach marketing at Colgate, and bought one of the loveliest homes they'd ever seen in nearby Latham, and a steal, at that.

David boxed up the remaining paint samples. "He's probably coming just to be sure I haven't set up my own advertising agency to pirate his clients—although after what he pulled, I think I'd be well within my rights."

They walked back to the kitchen area to wash up. The kitchen, along with the bathrooms, had been dismantled years earlier to accommodate code restrictions for public buildings. Among other things, the house had once been a Christian Science resource center.

When Abbie and David closed three weeks earlier, there were only two "restrooms" and a utility kitchen equipped with nothing more than a mini-fridge and an oversized stainless-steel sink. The contractor had already completed most of the renovation and, along with painting, was to start the rest of the work the next morning. Abbie was excited about the possibilities for the finished product—since setting eyes on the house, she had rekindled her dream of running a bed and breakfast.

For their lunch with Alton Deaver, Abbie had ordered boxed take-outs from Harriet's, a café in town famous for great sandwiches. Their hope was that eating in these uncomfortable, unadorned surroundings, with a floor half-covered in paint-splattered tarps, would help guarantee Deaver's early departure.

At a little past noon, they heard a car pull into the port cochere at the front entrance. They looked at each other and took a deep breath as Deaver's driver, Mason, stepped out of the black Lincoln limousine, walked around to the passenger side, and open the back door. Alton Deaver stepped out, his tanned, spa-polished skin one shade darker than his blazer, shirt collar open, no tie.

Abbie grunted. "I see he's in his best slumming mode."

They watched him thoughtfully take in the surroundings before he approached the heavy, wooden double doors with their vintage cameo of pastel colored stained glass. When he finally rang the bell, they stalled before answering.

"Holy Jeez, this is some place," Deaver said. "You didn't say anything about it being a small mansion." He gave David a strong hug and a slap on the back. Abbie quickly extended her hand, deflecting a similar greeting.

"Very good to see you both," Deaver said, looking from one to the other, then slowly gave the place the once-over with a keen eye. "Very good."

"Thank you," Abbie said. She had promised to use restraint. She had never cared for Deaver. Happily, her interaction with him over the years had been limited to a quarterly dinner foursome with his snooty, obsessive wife, Madeline, the company Christmas party and the summer picnic. Abbie had found him to be a very generous man when it favored his self-interest, and quite adept at using his immense wealth to punish, coerce or appease.

"How was the drive up?" David asked.

"Beautiful," said Deaver. "It only took a little over two hours."

They had set up a card table and three folding chairs in what probably was a study at one time, a large, handsome room with mahogany molding and deep rose-colored textured wallpaper.

A gold-brushed torchiere had been left there presumably by the previous owners.

"I wish you'd let me take you out for a nice lunch," Deaver said, opening his pink and yellow carton from Harriet's. "Not that this isn't nice. You know what I mean."

Abbie brought in a pitcher of iced tea and a cinnamon swirl pound cake from Pascale's, already a favorite of theirs in town.

"Things are a lot simpler here," David said. He looked over at Abbie. "We like it."

Deaver nodded. "What's not to like. When do I get the tour?"

"Well," Abbie jumped in, "you can see what a mess everything is."

"Do I care? This place is amazing. So is the whole town. I had Mason do a quick run through. I also Googled it. Beautiful. Who can resist tree-lined streets? Maples. The works. The per capita here is very impressive too. The shops have been in business an average of nine years with a rate of about two new businesses opening every quarter. You two really did your homework."

They really hadn't. They'd discovered the town through a local realtor the weekend they drove up to the school to discuss David's position. They'd heard of Latham, but had never known anything about it except that it was considered to be a nice place to live, was still growing and had an excellent school system. Although they didn't have children, and didn't plan to, they knew how important the school situation was for resale value.

It was love at first sight and once they knew those few important basics, Abbie had only three questions for the realtor: *Did anyone ever die in the house?* No. *Did anything horrible ever happen here?* No. *Is the house said to be haunted?* No. And off they went, content to learn the rest of its colorful history along the way.

Deaver removed an envelope from his inside jacket pocket, then draped the jacket over the back of his chair. "For you," he said, handing the envelope to David.

David took the envelope and set it on the table. "Thanks."

"No, no, open it now," Deaver said, almost child-like.

David slit open the envelope with his plastic table knife and removed a thin packet of folded papers. There was no check. "I don't understand. You indicated we were squaring up…that you were bringing my final check."

"I hate that word *final*, David. That's not a word for us. We've been together too long. You could be my nephew." He gestured to the document. "Look at the papers."

Abbie felt her jaw tighten. She glanced down at her plate and pushed cake crumbs around with her fork.

David looked over the two pages. "This is a contract."

"And…?" said Deaver.

"And what? You owe me $200,000."

"And…" Deaver went on, undeterred, "how much is the contract for?"

"It doesn't matter what the contract is for. I'm done, Alton. I thought I made that clear to you."

"How can you say it doesn't matter? I'm nearly doubling your salary and upping your annual bonus by thirty-five percent. It's right there, and I'm giving you your $200,000…"

"As a sign-up bonus." David cut in. "Are you kidding me? All I want from you is what I earned before you gave my two biggest clients to Suter. Why don't you understand that?"

"New associates are important. You don't need those clients. I have bigger and better things in store for you and me. Much bigger." Deaver leaned closer. "Come back, David."

"Does the name Rightman ring a bell, Alton? Does it? Two years ago, you did the same thing to me with Rightman Industries, the company's biggest account, my account. You used it as a bargaining chip to close the deal with Sid. And even that wasn't the first time. More than once I let you talk me out of leaving. Not this time."

Abbie cleared her throat and stood. "Hey, if we're going on the grand tour, we'd better get started or you'll hit all the rush hour traffic on the way back."

"How do you get along with no furniture?" Deaver asked, as they strolled the rooms.

"It's in storage," Abbie said. "We're staying at a bed and breakfast in town. The woman gave us a great rate. People here are nice."

Abbie and David walked Alton to the front of the one-story country French structure where there were two sitting areas, one to the left and one to the right upon entering, each opening to a larger room at the far side. Other rooms opened along the wide corridor, and everywhere, a vista of windows, light and trees.

Deaver followed along, nodding thoughtfully, but said nothing.

"There's maid's quarters down that way," David said, motioning casually.

For fear of prolonging Deaver's visit, David did not mention the enormous basement, with its three individual rooms, a few stainless steel worktables and a walk-in refrigerator the size of a small bedroom, most unusual. The realtor had volunteered that during a relatively brief period in its history, the building had been a speak-easy. The fact that bootleggers had mixed booze in the basement explained the numerous floor drains and the slightly pungent aroma.

"You know," said Deaver, after his long silence, "this is another world from another time. Special. Idyllic. When was the last time you saw a four-car garage?" He turned to David and cocked his head sympathetically. "Now tell me I didn't take good care of you." He gestured to the expanse of space. "I think it's fair to say you've done well by me these seven years."

"Eight," said Abbie, straight-faced. "Eight years of long hours and hard work. Let's give David some credit. You had a creative genius on your payroll."

"Seven, eight. Those years are behind us, Abbie. I'm offering David the fruitful years ahead. It's for both of you."

Abbie fought back screaming *thief, liar, creep.*

"What do you say?" Deaver waited.

Abbie could see the vein thickening in her husband's neck, something she had seen time and again during those eight years, but not once since moving to Latham.

"We've just given you a tour of our new home," David said, with an edge to his voice. "Does that mean anything to you?"

"Does it mean anything? Are you kidding me? This place is gorgeous. It's one of a kind. The style, the architectural appointments, six-inch crown molding. Nooks and alcoves. Fantastic."

"Thank you," Abbie said, stoic.

Deaver took a few steps, paused for a long moment facing away from them, then turned. "Let me buy it from you."

Abbie and David laughed. It was a proud moment. David put his arm around Abbie's shoulder.

"I'm serious." Deaver said. He moved in close. "Sell it to me. I'll give you three times what you paid for it."

"You're crazy," David said.

Abbie laughed. "You've got to be kidding."

"Look at me, David. You know me better than anybody. Do I look like I'm kidding?" David knew that look. He'd seen it with every account they'd ever landed, every deal they'd ever closed. Deaver would take in lots of information, like ingredients in a stock pot. He would quietly process, and when it was soup, he would get that look. It was a look that meant he knew exactly what he wanted to do next, and expected to get what he wanted.

Deaver looked around. "I wish there were some chairs so we could sit. I want to explain…"

"There's nothing to explain, Alton."

Abbie stiffened. "It's out of the question."

"Madeline…" Deaver started and sighed. "Madeline is very upset with me right now, and I can't seem to make it up to her. She's starting to shut me out."

David put up his hands. "I don't know what this has to do with us or this house, but…"

"Just listen to me, please David. Abbie."

Abbie put her head back and felt the tightness building in her shoulders. The last thing in the world she wanted was to hear about Deaver's marital relationship. Madeline Deaver, seventeen years her husband's junior, broke up Deaver's second marriage. Abbie found her to be as self-absorbed as her husband. They had met four years earlier at the Hyatt, where Abbie was working as a front desk manager. Even back then, she had a reputation for being an opportunist and a Class-A snob.

Now, along with her diamonds, the third Mrs. Deaver wore a constant thin smile that lacked any warmth or sentiment. She had people to write her thank you notes and even sign them for her. She bragged about the four hundred pairs of shoes in her two-story walk-in closet that required a rolling ladder.

When she was out of her element, everything bothered her. At the annual picnic, she became squeamish about the sand, the lack of convenience, the occasional fly, the possibility of soil of any kind. She sniffed as though the very air was a bother. She would incessantly brush at her toenails to make sure her pedicure was still intact. Noise offended her. People talking to her offended her. Ordinary life offended her. Everything was foul.

"I love that woman," said Deaver. "You've never heard me talk like this, but it's true. She's everything to me."

Well, not everything, Abbie thought. *Otherwise how could one account for…let's see…Vanessa, the young woman who brought over the contracts for all his copy machines, Charlene, the accounting intern. Then there was Bambi – Lord, was there actually a Bambi?*

"She's always talking about a country place, a get-away," Deaver continued. "She would love it here and she would fit right in. The town has class. The house will be pristine. You know how finicky she is. If I could give her this house as a gift…you know…surprise her, I know everything would be okay. She would realize how much I care. I would be her hero again."

"My God, you're serious," Abbie ran her fingers through her hair. Were there no limits in this horrible man's narcissistic little world?

"Absolutely out of the question, Alton," David said. He had begun pacing. "What's wrong with the Hamptons. Buy her something in the Hamptons."

"The Hamptons? The Hamptons isn't what it used to be. It's just another version of the city. There's no country on the Island anymore, you know that."

"Be that as it may, Alton, you have my answer." David took

Abbie's hand. "Our answer."

"Four times. I'll give you four times what you paid. Just give me a number."

"We think not," said Abbie.

"Then, please, keep thinking," said Deaver. "This place isn't for the two of you. You're city people like me."

David looked at Abbie. "Not anymore."

"Well, I'm leaving everything on the table—the contract, the offer on the house…"

"Not everything, Alton. My check for $200,000 isn't on the table. Please don't make me turn this over to a lawyer."

Deaver put his hands together, prayer-like, in front of him. "David, David, I would never make you do such a thing. I would never make you go up against our legal team. I wouldn't even want to go up against our legal team." He placed his hand gently against David's chest and lowered his voice almost to a whisper. "Have you ever known them to lose?"

"Well, then, there really is nothing more to discuss, is there?" David said.

A few minutes later, Deaver headed out the door. Before getting into the limo, he turned and smiled. "Call me. Love you both."

Back inside, Abbie shook her head and sat exhausted on the floor. "Can you flipping believe that crazy, horrible cretin?

"I can't," said David. "I thought I could never again be surprised by anything he did."

"Do you for one minute believe that whole Madeline

thing?"

David sat down beside her and managed a chuckle. "Oh, he wants Madeline up here all right. He wants a nice place to park her while he has his little flings in the city."

"Well, what goes around comes around. Madeline broke up his second marriage. She's not a nice person."

"No, she is not," David said. "Deaver's secretary…you remember Molly…she was telling me that right after the divorce, Alton's ex went back to the house to retrieve a very expensive emerald bracelet that she'd forgotten in the bedroom safe, and Madeline wouldn't give it to her. And if that wasn't bad enough—you know what a finicky pain in the ass Madeline is. She wouldn't dream of wearing somebody else's bracelet— germs and all that—so she sold it and bought something new for herself. That's about as low as it gets."

Abbie shook her head. "What a pair. They deserve each other. They're both thieves."

"You know what I'm thinking right now?"

"That we're out $200,000?" Abbie gave a wry chuckle.

"I'm thinking how grateful I am for you and for our life together." He leaned over and kissed her on the cheek.

"Any regrets?"

"Not a one. And who knows, there might be a bed and breakfast in your future, after all."

"I can't believe we snatched it off the market before anybody else."

David became pensive. "I know this is going to sound odd,

but I can't help feeling sorry for Deaver. He has so much, but he's never satisfied with anything."

"I have trouble feeling sorry for him, David. Alton Deaver is a selfish, wicked man married to a selfish, wicked woman."

"Maybe that's all the more reason to pity him. I guess I just feel sorry for a guy who has no idea what true happiness or true love is really about."

A few days after Alton Deaver's visit, they had another visitor. This one was most unexpected.

The house buzzed with the contractor's crew, painting, mixing grout, removing wallpaper, hauling tiles and tubs and two-by-fours. Kitchen cabinets were installed, granite set in place.

The front doors stood wide open to the fresh air of the late April afternoon, and when she walked in no one even noticed her at first. She stood for a few minutes at the entry, turning here and there, obviously baffled by the chaotic goings on. One of the workmen caught sight of her and mentioned it to Abbie.

"Can I help you?" Abbie asked as she side-stepped all the clutter on her way to the front doors.

The woman was small and frail and appeared confused, her frightened eyes darting from one corner to another. She wore a neat, dark print dress, and black cotton gloves. Her left arm was cocked to accommodate the handle of her black leather purse. Abbie wasn't sure if the woman had heard her.

"May I help you?" Abbie said again, this time a bit louder and more pronounced.

"I've come to see Howard," said the lady. Her voice quivered. "I've come to see my Howard." She held a small white eyelet handkerchief in her right hand.

"I'm afraid there is no one here by that name," Abbie said. "What address were you looking for? Maybe I can help you find it."

"I've come to see Howard," she said, clearly agitated. "Fifty-one years together and now I can't find him."

"But there's no one here by that name. You must be looking for another address. If you tell me what it is, I might be able to help you find him."

The woman ignored Abbie and started walking toward the center hallway.

Abbie called after her, "Please. Wait." The woman kept walking. Her steps were small and deliberate.

Abbie caught up with her, and gently took her arm. "I'm very concerned you might fall. There's a lot of work going on here, as you can see. And, honestly, Howard is not here."

"Howard is right in there," said the woman, pointing to the room on the other side of the center doors.

"Here," Abbie said, "let me show you. We'll walk very carefully."

The woman's tiny arm felt boney in Abbie's careful grasp. Once on the other side of the doors, the woman pointed to the room on the left. "Here it is. Here's where my Howard is," she said. Her voice had brightened, confident in her accuracy.

Abbie led her a few steps into the room, which was empty except for ladders, paint cans and tarps. The woman's eyes grew wide. A look of panic crossed her face. She pressed her handkerchief to her mouth and wailed. "He's gone. My Howard is gone," she cried. "What have you done with him? What have you done with my Howard?"

Before Abbie could say anything, there was another voice. Abbie turned to see a stout, dark-skinned woman enter the room.

"It's all right, Mildred," the woman said. She took the elderly lady by the arm and turned to Abbie. "Please excuse our intrusion, Mrs. Birch."

"She must be looking for another address." Abbie wondered how this woman knew her name. "Have we met?"

"No," said the woman, smiling. "You must not be accustomed to living in a small town. Word has gotten around there are new owners here. I'm Mrs. Lucia Perez from Trinity Senior Living, several blocks away." She extended her hand to Abbie. "And this lovely if sometimes naughty lady is Mildred Coharren, one of our residents. She's done this twice before. I do apologize."

"It's no problem," Abbie said. "Is Howard her husband?"

"He was. He passed away about a year ago and..."

"Hey," David called out cheerfully, as he came around the corner into the hallway. "I didn't know we had company. Who've we got here? I'm David Birch."

Abbie introduced both women, and explained about Mrs. Coharren, who was still desperately preoccupied with finding her husband.

"Oh, that's too bad," said David. "Is there anything we can do to help?"

"I'm afraid not," said Mrs. Perez, "and I do sincerely apologize. Understandably, she keeps wanting to return to the place she last saw him. I hope we won't be bothering you again. Best of luck to you both." She took Mrs. Coharren by the arm and turned to leave. "Come, Mildred, we'll have a nice cup of tea."

"I want my Howard," was all Mrs. Coharren said through her tears.

David and Abbie gave each other a puzzled look.

"Had they lived here?" Abbie asked. "Why would this have been the last place she saw him?"

"That's when it was still Stark's," said Mrs. Perez.

"Stark's?"

"The funeral home."

The words landed like a sledge hammer. Abbie threw her hand to her mouth.

"I…I don't think we understand," said David, feeling as if his heart and stomach had just traded places.

"You didn't know?"

Alton Deaver was beside himself with joy when David

called to give him the good news. "I knew it," said Deaver. "I knew you'd come through for me, David. You have saved my marriage."

Two weeks later, the deal was final. David apologized to Colgate and accepted a job at SUNY Albany, seventy miles farther away from New York City. Deaver made good on his offer and gave Abbie and David four times what they had paid for the house, in addition to the $200, 000 that he owed David. It pleased Deaver immensely to be able to surprise Madeline. And, once Abbie and David got over their initial shock and disappointment at the extraordinary turn of events, they too delighted immensely in Alton Deaver's surprise for his darling Madeline.

A Christmas Surprise

I SAW MOMMY kissing Santa Claus. I laughed every time I heard those lyrics because they were true. I did see Mommy kissing Santa. As the song says, they didn't see me sneak down the stairs to have a peek. I had decided to go down one last time to make sure Santa's Toll House Cookies were in just the right place. I had helped my mom make them.

And there they were. It was a long, slow kiss. I had seen a kiss like that in a movie, but I never saw real people do it. Mom was all wrapped up in Santa's arms. I heard her moan and giggle quietly. I felt so proud that Santa thought my mother, of all mothers, was so special. I enjoyed that thought very privately, like a good little boy. I didn't want to hurt my dad's feelings. I didn't know if he ever kissed Mom like that or if he ever made her moan and giggle that way.

I loved my mom and dad. Each morning, Mom fixed us breakfast, while Dad sat reading the paper at the kitchen table. He always had work things on his mind and never said very much. Before leaving the house, he mussed my hair in fun and gave Mom a little kiss on the cheek. Except for the sound of bacon sizzling in the skillet, those were quiet mornings. And peaceful.

Things weren't always that way. Sometimes, I'd hear Mom and Dad arguing late at night. They sounded angry. Doors slammed, and sometimes I thought I heard Mom crying. But in the morning, things would be back to normal—Mom was at the stove and Dad was at the kitchen table with his paper.

One Christmas, I overheard my mom tell a friend she was sure my dad was going to surprise her with a cruise to the Bahamas. She had been dropping hints about it for weeks. We never took vacations. My dad was too busy with work. He was a tax accountant and had his own business. He did very well. We lived in a nice house and Mom had a cleaning woman come in once a week. Dad bought a new car every other year, the one he liked best, but always insisted Mom pick out the color.

Every year for Christmas, Mom gave Dad things he loved. One year she gave him season hockey tickets. Boy, did he like those. Another year, she got him the special sound system he'd been hinting about. Dad liked to give Mom jewelry, although she never wore it much. I don't think Mom liked jewelry. She never did get the cruise to the Bahamas.

The arguing became louder and more frequent. I was scared because a boy in my class told me his mom and dad used to yell and fight all the time. They finally got a divorce and he hardly ever saw his dad much after that.

But the following year, my mom and dad stopped arguing.

I remember it very clearly. I was six. That was the year I saw Mommy kissing Santa Claus. Of course, I didn't know who Santa was back then. Later on, I realized that Mom and Dad had managed to work things out. Mom smiled a lot more. She often hummed while making our breakfast. Our home was happy again. Mom was happy. Dad seemed quite satisfied with things. It had all started with that kiss. I never let on that I had seen them that Christmas Eve. I was just glad they'd worked it out.

They had even worked out the whole vacation issue. Once a year, my dad took us all on a trip. That first year, we went camping in the Adirondacks. The next, we went to Disneyland. He also arranged for my mom to have two vacations a year on her own. Apparently, this was something Mom had asked for. She said she liked quiet time away to refresh from her hectic schedule at home. It pleased Dad too, because while she was away he could get a lot of paperwork done and still have time left over for a round of golf. At last, everything was fine and dandy.

The Christmas when I was fifteen, my dad and I went out early in the morning to a tree farm about twenty miles from our house. Mom sent us off with a smile and a thermos of hot cocoa. I had never felt happier. We walked the fragrant evergreen rows and it didn't take me long to find just the tree I wanted. It was a beautiful Fraser fir with long arching branches, just like the old-fashioned kind I'd seen on Christmas cards. But Dad thought we could find a better one. He always liked things to be as perfect as they could be. It took a while longer to find just the right tree to make Dad happy.

"This is a tree we can be proud of," was what he said. Dad often talked about being proud of things. When company came, I could see how proud he was showing them new things he and Mom had gotten for the house. He was proud of all his electronics, his new car and his big ride-on mower. I knew he was always proud of Mom and me. He would ask Mom to show off the latest piece of jewelry he'd gotten her. Sometimes he became impatient when she took too long to find it. Dad had often criticized her for not wearing the jewelry he gave her.

"If you had any idea what this cost," he'd say, "you would take better care of it."

I helped Dad fasten the tree to the top of the car and enjoyed a cup of Mom's hot cocoa. It was a cold morning and the sky was heavy with the milky gray of oncoming snow. As we headed home, Dad turned on the radio. A CD started playing.

"'The Savvy Negotiator.' You can learn something from this, son."

It was Christmas and I wasn't in the mood to learn anything. Mom would have a big breakfast waiting for us when we got home. Life was good. "Can we put on some Christmas music?" I asked.

"Life can't always be about music and play things, Son. You've got to be aware of what's happening in the world around you. Learn what's going on. Get savvy." But he reluctantly agreed.

To my surprise, Jimmy Boyd was the first voice we heard. *I Saw Mommy Kissing Santa Claus.* It had become my favorite because of that special memory—Dad dressed up as Santa, Mom all wrapped up in his arms.

"Wouldn't it be fun to get out the old Santa suit and surprise Mom?" I said, laughing.

"What Santa suit?"

"Your Santa suit. The one you used to wear on Christmas Eve."

"I never had a Santa suit."

"Yes, you did. I saw you." I rolled my eyes. "It's okay, Dad, I'm fifteen. You can tell me now."

"That wasn't me, Son. I thought you knew by now. That was Mr. Mitchell. He was the one who always played Santa for all you kids in the neighborhood. I never had time for that sort of thing."

I felt my heart drop like it was tied to a rock. "Mr. Mitchell? From three houses down?"

"Yup. Dan Mitchell. Heck of a guy," Dad said, "even if he is a little too easy-going for my taste." He laughed. "Who ever heard of a grown man taking a couple of vacations a year? By himself! Who does that? Silly, right? Anyway, I figured by now you'd have known he was your Santa. Hope I haven't burst your bubble."

"Mr. Mitchell?" was all I could say, as my world tipped slowly on its side. The rest of the way home, neither one of us said another word.

The Man on the Hill

MID-AFTERNOON, THE MAN made his way up the hill, a small drum fastened to his waistband, then paused amid the familiar stony landscape. He'd been walking since dawn until, finally, he could see it, the dark cluster of gatherers off in the distance. So, it was true after all. It was true.

He dropped his head, his anguish nearly unbearable.

When the news had first reached him, he couldn't believe what he was hearing. He knew these people. How long ago was it exactly? Thirty years…more or less? He clearly remembered the day the woman had given birth. He was just a boy himself, yet he would never forget the moment. After that, he had seen the family from time to time passing through the village. But mostly it was the boy. Such an unusual child. People would gather around him. His mother cautioned him many times, but he had such a compelling way about him and was very headstrong. Loving, but headstrong. And she was so understanding, even though she had a look in her eye, a look, oddly, not so much of fearfulness as of a kind of desolate resignation.

The boy was determined. And the older he got, the more determined he became until he angered many people by the things that he said and did. More than once, there was violence. But he would just move on as if nothing had happened, though not oblivious to the dangers that often surrounded him.

The man continued up the hill, having to stop unexpectedly for a short while when a sudden raging sky brought the fiercest of gales and lightning, as if the world itself were being ripped apart. He'd had to duck down deep amid the rocks with his hands over his head to protect himself. But soon, an eerie calmness fell over the place.

At the top of the hill, at the very top, it was all so painfully clear. He could not look away. Yet, he could not fathom what had taken place here. He fell to his knees, eyes stinging from the salt of his tears and bowed his head in prayer.

After a few moments, he rose and turned to face the woman at his side. He saw again that same look of desolate resignation, this time at the sight of her son nailed there upon a cross. The man lifted his drum and the woman nodded, as she once had done all those many years ago in that little stable where he had gone to play for the newborn King. Now, there were no ox and lambs to keep time, only the taps of a mournful cadence.

Jeremiah's Orchard

ON A BEAUTIFUL burnt-golden afternoon in the fall of 1952, the town of Early suffered a monumental, life-changing calamity. Before then, I had only thought my father to be an extraordinary man, but on that fateful day, within the space of a few astonishing moments, I knew without a doubt that it was so. I cannot tell you what I would have done in his place. I can only say that from that time forward, Jeremiah Hendrik was a legend.

My dad grew up in Early, as did his dad and granddad, and more Hendriks before them. Ours was a valley town in that part of the northeast where the terraced hillsides displayed, in opulent profusion, the apple orchards that had passed through generations of the families that owned them, ours among them.

As a boy, I walked the orchard with my dad, through the rows fragrant with the simple pure sweetness of Golden Delicious tinged with the mild vinous acidity of McIntosh. Those were the money crops, but I always sensed a quiet pride he had in his rare, lesser-known and vintage varieties, which had little to no mass appeal – the Ballarat Seedlings and Beeley Pippins, along with the drab but pear-sweet Ashmead Kernel, a grower's pleasure.

He seemed to know every leaf on every tree, eight hundred trees in all, many as old as fifty years, every one put in the ground by a Hendrik. Some were by his own hand, saplings or grafted stock, often replacing ones that had died off from freeze, fire blight or winter burn.

I followed along as he plucked the misshapen apples that would not do well at market. Routinely, he removed dozens of perfectly fine young apples as well. "We have to sacrifice these, son," he had taught me, "so the ones that remain have more nutrients."

Whether by nature or arduous circumstance, no one was a more dedicated man than my dad. An outsider might say he was a good businessman who lived for the harvest. I saw that he was simply a good man who lived for the beauty of creation, nature's perpetual timing, and the tradition of touching things touched by those who went before.

"You can't make an apple on an assembly line," he would say, humble in the notion that he had been granted, through no warranting of his own, the stewardship of a great and glorious piece of fertile hillside, a duty whose blessing he saw as beyond measure.

My mom did not grow up in our way of life. She came from a family of teachers, as she herself was, but she fit so well into the tradition that she saw her own duty in all of it. She knew the challenges that came with marrying a grower. "And a fine one at that," she would say, well aware of her blessings.

The town of Early officially came about with the building of the Great High Dam decades and decades back. Before then, in my great grandfather's youth, the place was nothing more than a scattering of small wooden buildings along the water's edge. A general store, a tavern, a smithy, a bank, and a popular eatery named Fish's, after Fish Bennett, Early's first attorney, justice of the peace and mayor.

The center of town was the little white church that doubled as the schoolhouse. In time, there was the old auction house, called that even when it was new, a few storage barns and a wagon maker. Then came the cider house, the first major employer in the area.

Once the Great High Dam was put in place to hold back the often-crazy waters of the Arkine River, the valley came alive with commerce and local culture, and Early started having two of everything … two banks, two dry goods stores, two taverns, and two eateries. With all that came Early's first haberdashery.

People began moving into the area, and they, along with others who had been in these parts for years, came to town for leisure things such as the new movie house and the town hall that had a stage where someone once came to "play act" Abraham Lincoln. That's when Early got its first library, small as it was, in the back of Harris Kewly's boot shop. That's also when the Early Funeral Parlor expanded and the more fashionable "May We" Hair Styling Salon opened for business.

The Funeral Parlor later changed its name, since it made folks uncomfortable to see the words "early" and "funeral" alongside each other.

It was during that time, generations back, that townsfolk thought up the idea of an annual festival to correspond with the end of the fall apple-picking season. No one possibly could have foretold what profound significance this would someday have for us all.

In these parts the weather was predictable, the worst of it an occasional mild fury that frightened the animals and gave the growers only momentary cause for alarm. Every now and then, there would be what townsfolk called "an atmospheric anomaly," such as occurred in the winter of 1936, when the ocean froze off the coast of Maine. That extraordinary season of ripping wind and ice marked the end of the Baldwin apple throughout the region. But all of that would pale compared to the calamity of 1952.

"A life lived in harvest years can be a hard life, son," my dad would say to me, remembering, in particular, one piercing blow of lightning that had hung in the sky like a clothesline before exploding on a 100-year-old shade tree, splitting it apart and setting it ablaze. The wind-driven flames took my grandfather's barn and everything in it, including the season's yield.

My dad was just a boy then, but he would forever recall with gratitude how townsfolk, young and old alike, women with babies in arms, scurried up desperately from the valley.

They formed brigades on the hillside, hitched up hoses to water wagons where they could, and passed buckets to do what turned out to be the impossible task of settling the fire

The following month, my grandfather suffered a mild stroke. For the next two years, he worked the orchard with my dad alongside, but finally succumbed. Those next years were especially challenging. "Building things back is harder than keeping them up," my dad always said. He and my grandmother managed to hold things together, and when my dad reached the legal age to make decisions, she turned over the reins to him.

The orchard was my father's livelihood and life. Everyone could see that aside from my mom and me, there was nothing more important to Jeremiah Hendrik than the orchard. We lived a life of comfort with none of the showiness. Our Ford pick-up wasn't new, but it ran fine and looked good. Our two-story white clapboard house was big and homey with a white porch railing and a cornflower-blue glider swing that my dad had made one year as a Christmas surprise for my mom and me.

We had all we needed and we were grateful, more so in that particular year—the year, coincidentally, that was to change everything—because my dad had finally built the barn he had dreamed of, planned on and worked for, for so many years. As fate would have it, his joy was to be short-lived.

The barn was a great handsome two-story wooden structure with a steep slanted roof and 10 small square windows. I had watched them set the sturdy oak beams in place and fit out the roomy interior with stainless-steel equipment, new refrigeration, sorting belts and heavy-duty crates, palettes and bins.

My dad had long dreamed about it—that one proud and special place that housed most of what he needed to turn our farm into a modern apple operation.

In that very year, the year I turned 12, my dad got an offer on the farm. He wasn't the first; big corporations had moved into the region, buying up old family-run orchards. Three serious looking men in dark suits came to our house more than once, upping their offer each time. They had mistaken my dad's unwavering sense of tradition and love of the land for a ploy to get more money. It took them a while to see that there was no price tempting enough for Jeremiah Hendrik.

Even Varnal Person, my dad's lifelong friend, gave in to the promise of having more money than he had ever had in his entire life. That promise served Varnal well, but it was not the prospect of money that appealed to my father.

"Are you sure you realize what you're turning down, Jer'miah?" Varnal had asked during that turbulent time when the Selly-Mortine Corporation was in hot pursuit. My dad had many friends, but outside of my mom and me, no one was closer to him than Varnal Person. Their fathers and their fathers' fathers had known each other well. They also had grown up in the orchards and gone to school together.

"Times are changing," Varnal said, as he sat with my mom

and dad around our kitchen table. In the quiet of the upstairs hall, I had listened hard on those nights as he made his heartfelt case.

"You're worried for me, Varnal, and you ought not to be," I heard my dad say.

"I worry as family worries, Jer'miah, for the folks they care about the most. You and Olive and William could make a new way. You'd have enough money to do anything in this whole wide world that you cared to."

"We do that now," said my dad. And that was the end of it.

Varnal built a big fancy house in the valley and took Mrs. Person to Paris, France. When they got back he set her up in the business she had only dreamed about, and Mrs. Adelaide Person became proprietress of Early's first bridal shop, Madame Adelaide's Salon for Brides. Madame Adelaide's was located at the bottom of the very mountain where Varnal's family had toiled proudly in the orchard for six generations.

In that particular year, all the talk was about the Apple Festival. The season had been a prosperous one for most, and the town was riding high with enough money to put on the best festival we'd ever had. For months, the Festival Committee had made their plans and purchases, and now in the few weeks leading up to the big weekend, the valley resembled a colony of ants, all of them on purpose, draping bright leaf garlands and stringing ropes of little white lights that would trace the town like drops of moonlight.

Colorful square booths for food and crafts and arcade

games lined the park near the center of town. Signs fashioned in the customary excellence of Lafitte's Printing were hung to mark each one. Police readied the barricades that would close off side roads for the big event. Now and then, from every corner of Early, you could hear the trumpet strains of the school marching bands rehearsing for their big moment.

It was in these last many hours that an event of a very different kind was taking form far up the valley—an event that would demand of us more than some would say was reasonable to give.

It never failed to please my dad to see townsfolk busily engaged in the annual Festival. "William," he often liked to say, "there are no finer people anywhere than right here in Early." He said it with pride as he glanced down the valley from our high hilltop. That's when he would muss my hair, letting me know I was one of them and that I too, could be proud as he. I was.

As I look back, it amazes me how well people organized things in spite of their limited communications. Many townsfolk did not have telephones, and those who did relied on the central operators, Tilly, Merle and Hope, to put their calls through.

The postman came to the front door with special delivery letters, and sometimes the side door by the kitchen when he smelled fresh-baked pie. A telegram arrived for urgent matters. Mostly, people were out and about and saw each other shopping or at Church or just doing a day's work, and passed the word about this or that. And things got said and things got done, much of it useful to our way of life. It's what we did in those days and in those parts.

Like many people in business, we had a telephone, but up there on high ground we were just remote enough to lose signal or hear crackled sounds that often scratched out every other word. It was what they called a "party line" system because you could end up in someone else's conversation without meaning to or just pick up fragments of other voices. One minute my mom would be talking with Mrs. Buchanan and the next minute she would hear Essie Millbauer over at Glenda's Florals.

"I don't know what we would do," my mom sometimes said, "if we had to really depend on this thing." She could not have known how very close she was to finding out.

This, the biggest festival year of them all, was the first ever that my mom would miss. She was headed 65 miles away to Pillsbury for her 20-year college reunion. She had majored in English and became a teacher, as did many of her friends. My mom was good at keeping in touch with people. Many times I would find her at the little antique secretary that sat in the hall at the foot of the staircase, writing on her flowered notepaper and smiling that kind of dreamy, contented smile that comes with good memories and wistfulness.

Mom being away meant time for just me and my dad, time mostly out in the new barn, which was now our favorite place. It had an important look about it and a smell of newly cut wood and metal polish. In the morning sunlight that streamed

through the few windows, the stainless steel shone like a mirror.

"Things in their place and a good place at that," my dad would say. "The Lord's been good to us, Will." He was at once proud of and humbled by the barn he had waited so long for.

With my mom away, it was the perfect time to work on replacing the truck's carburetor, which for several hours would render us without a vehicle. We had no way of knowing how this single circumstance would figure mightily into the unfolding of the extraordinary events of that day.

The first of it came several hours after my mom had driven off. We'd been out in the barn trying to finish up so we could have the truck ready to make our way down the mountain for the opening ceremonies at 4:00. It had been our tradition that Varnal and Adelaide would come by for us and we would all go together. Now that they lived in the valley, we would make our way down on our own and meet them there.

We came around the porch and heard the telephone, but by the time we made it through the door, the ringing had stopped. We knew it wasn't my mom because she had already signaled us with two short sets of rings that she had arrived safely in Pillsbury—long distance calls were an extravagance.

As we washed up, the telephone rang again. "I'll bet that's Varnal," my dad said. "Probably wants to firm up plans where to meet." I picked up the receiver, but there was only the weak hint of a man's voice amid the crackling. I looked at my dad, shrugged and shook my head.

"One of these days," he said, "someone's bound to invent a

better telephone line." They surely would, but not in time for the town of Early.

The day itself was about as fine and beautiful a fall day as any I could recall. One year the frost had come so soon in the season that many folks couldn't stay through the evening for the fireworks and opening night concert. But on this brilliant late September day, even the trees did their part with a fiery-redness that lit the hills around us.

Calls soon rang in once or twice again, but the connection hadn't improved. Quiet as it was on our high ground, we could hear the building of voices in laughter and high spirits amid the broken strains of final trumpet practice and the occasional thunder of drums.

"Do you suppose Mrs. Edewine will make her Swedish brittle this year?"

"You bet she will," said my dad, confident in his hope of enjoying what many women in town, including my mom, had tried and failed to duplicate.

The phone rang again and I was able to clearly hear a man's excited voice.

"Jer'miah?" he called out loud and breathless. I handed the phone to my dad.

Dad listened and went white. "Lord have mercy, Carl," he said, and listened some more. "My truck's out of commission," he said at last. "I'll have to do something else. How much time do we have?"

I had never seen my dad look scared. When he hung up, he

ran for the door with me close behind.

"The Great High's been breached. The State Police can't reach anyone. The copter's on a medical airlift. We've got to warn them down there." He was frantic. "They've got to get to high ground."

I felt my heart beating in my ears. "Can't we take the tractor down? What if I run down? You know I can run fast."

"We'd never make it in time, son," he said, turning here and there for something that might provide a solution. "They've got to get out now. Ten minutes. Not much more. It's all we've got."

We stood at the edge of the hill and yelled at the top of our lungs, waving our arms high above our heads, but we were no match for the drumbeats and trumpet strains of the final band warm-up. Everyone was queued along the parade route. It was a high time for a town on the brink of catastrophe.

"Run and get the matches off the stove," he yelled, as he tore at the buttons of his flannel shirt. "And bring the broom."

When I rushed back, I saw that he had braced one of our wooden ladders against the side of the tractor. He climbed up and draped his shirt over the end of the broom, then set it on fire. He held out the broom as high as he could reach and waved it about.

It was no use. In the brilliance of the late afternoon sun, no one even noticed the flames. I was terrified now because of the town's peril and the desperation I saw in my father's face.

"Go in and call…call anyone, everyone," he shouted, "and keep calling."

I ran into the kitchen and frantically started dialing numbers from our phone book, my fingers trembling uncontrollably. A few minutes had already passed. I watched my dad through the window, and saw him stop cold. For a moment, he just stood there perfectly still. He put his hand to his mouth, as if in thought. I was puzzled and frightened. It was not apparent to me that he was remembering something.

As the number I called rang without answer, I saw him start running toward the barn. I hung up and ran out after him. The barn was about fifty yards from the house. By the time I got there, he was holding one of the large gas cans.

"Did you reach anyone?" he yelled. Six minutes had passed.

"No." I yelled back.

"Go back to the house and stay there."

"But I want to …"

"Go back, I said, and stay there."

I half-ran, half-walked, looking back over my shoulder. Then I stopped and turned around, stunned. He was starting to pour the gasoline around the outside of the barn. I ran back toward him.

"Dad! Dad! No!"

"Go back," he yelled.

He struck a match, tossed it onto the gasoline, and ran toward the house. A thunderous whoosh of flames shot up and across the side of the barn.

He opened the valve of one of the irrigation lines, then turned the hose on the house. When I caught up with him, he handed me the hose.

"Keep fanning the water," he said, as he ran to the edge of the hilltop.

I realized then how he had nobly re-enacted a piece of his father's history. I saw him watch as townsfolk, young and old alike, women with babies in arms, scurried up desperately from the valley. Fire trucks, already staged for the festival, barreled up the long hill road, sirens screaming. Trucks and cars followed in a stream. People stood on running boards and piled into pick-ups.

Jeremiah Hendrik watched and remembered as the thundering waters of the Arkine River, for so long captive in the once Great High Dam, were loosed upon the empty streets of Early.

Amid flags and bunting, streamers and balloons, debris of every sort pushed recklessly along in the rising current, slamming into clapboard houses and plowing through shop windows. The raging water lifted away cars and refrigerators and sent them tumbling onto front porches, which themselves soon floated off. Sewing machines and dining room tables swirled over rooftops.

In the dazzling sunlight of that late September afternoon, the gleaming brass trumpets bobbed past, hurried and silent. Great white billowy wedding gowns, their sleeves outstretched as if in total submission, floated helplessly along like angels who had lost their power to fly. To some, it might have looked as if a part of heaven itself were being washed away. But my dad knew better. As flames consumed the barn behind him, I watched him fall to his knees with tears and gratitude.

The Long Ride Home

"Where were you last night?" she asked, rising with a start as he came through the door of their North Square Street house. She had sat those many hours in the rocker near the hearth, waiting, her anxiety measured by the swiftness of her crochet hook. "I have been worried sick, Husband."

He took her hand. "Forgive me, Dearest Rachel. There's much to tell." He slipped his foot into the boot pull. "I'm spent."

Young Elizabeth ran to him and grabbed at his mud-stained trousers. He picked her up and kissed her cheek. "My sweetness," he whispered.

Rachel helped him out of his damp and heavy surcoat. "Have you eaten? I can warm the veal and pease pudding."

"Just tea." He washed his hands in the porcelain basin. "We were at John's relatives. They fed us."

He walked over to the cradle and, with his hand, touched a kiss to Joshua's forehead.

Rachel looked to the window, to the gray light of the chilly April morning. "I didn't hear you ride up."

"I came on foot." He hesitated, mindful of her fears. "I was detained. They kept my horse."

"Oh, Paul." She set down the silver teapot and leaned over, pressing her cheek against his. "I fear for you so."

He patted her arm.

"And what of the others?" she asked.

"There were casualties. Sam and John are fine. The soldiers came for them, but we managed to get them to safety." He lifted Elizabeth onto his lap.

Rachel poured their tea. "What if something had happened to you? There are seven children who need you. I need you."

He took her hand. "What ever would I have done without you, Dear Wife, the way you care for this little one and the others, as if they were your very own. Sarah—rest her soul— surely smiled down upon me and sent you into my life."

She gestured toward the cradle and smiled. "And now a second brood in the making."

"I promise you, Sweet Rachel, I will be here for them and for you."

"But each time you go out you risk everything. War is coming, Paul. I feel it." She drew a lace handkerchief from her pinafore and dabbed her eyes.

He put his daughter down and stood by the fire. "I'm afraid it already has."

Rachel turned to him, startled.

"I crossed the Charles last night," he said. "The Somerset was anchored there, but by the grace of God I passed unnoticed.

I arrived in Charlestown, then rode on, stopping at every farmhouse I could to warn them. Eventually, there were about forty riders. It was midnight before I connected with Sam and John at the home of Mrs. Hancock's parents in Lexington. We spent hours planning our next moves. It was after that that the British patrol picked me up."

"Thank God they released you."

He walked over to her and held her tight. "I fear it will be a hard road ahead. The Redcoats are well-trained and deliberate."

She looked up at him. "How can we possibly overcome a King's army?"

"We'll lose many patriots, good men all. But our militia is organized and determined—fiercely so. There's talk of a new gun, the long rifle, that may give us advantage. Most of all, we have men like Samuel Adams and John Hancock…"

"And you, Dear Husband." She kissed him.

"Pray, Mrs. Revere, that the Almighty would have us prevail."

She nodded, her eyes pressed shut for a moment. Then she took his hand. "Come. I'll fill the tub for your bath."

Madonna and Child

"You are one stubborn pest." Clare laughed, shaking her head at the woman who faced her across the counter.

"The answer is 'no' and it's going to stay 'no.'"

"But it's been up there for what…eight, nine years?"

"Nearly ten now, actually. And for all I know, Martie, it might be up there for ten more. I made a promise."

Martie Sanders put her hand on Clare's. "My dear friend, who's the stubborn one? You have no way of knowing if the woman is even still alive. And by the way, from what you told me, she didn't even seem to care about what you promised."

Clare's husband, George, came from the back room carrying a stack of small bright yellow shopping bags. "Save your breath, Martie. I've had this conversation with her half a dozen times in the last month alone." He stepped behind the counter and placed the bags on a shelf under the register.

Clare looked off into space. "I guess I just have a feeling about it. About something she said to me that day right before she rushed out of the store. I've never been able to forget it."

The shop had been busier than usual now that the snowbirds were returning and, as usual, this meant renewed interest in the figurine. "Oh, what about that one up there?" one customer had asked only the day before. "I've never seen one like it. It's gorgeous." The answer was the same as always. "So sorry, that piece isn't for sale."

"Look. I have an idea." Martie didn't appear ready to surrender. "Since you feel that strongly about it, why don't you just donate the money to a worthy cause. St. Jude maybe. Or Food for the Poor. Simon's Angels."

Clare slowly shook her head. "I just can't."

"Which reminds me." Martie turned and gestured toward the front window of the shop where a small poster advertised the ribbon-cutting for a drug rehab clinic, a celebratory fundraiser taking place the following week. "I bought you a ticket. Fifty dollars, my treat. It's a good cause."

"Not that I don't appreciate it," Clare said, straightening a tray of small antique silver dinner bells, "but I told you I might not be able to go if the store gets busy. Maybe you should consider inviting someone else." She looked at Martie. "But I am grateful for the thought."

A customer approached the counter to pay for two vintage teacups and a pewter candle snuffer. "I'm sorry. I couldn't help overhearing your conversation about that figurine." She pointed to the top shelf of the decorative etagere-like cabinet fixed to one end of the counter, facing in. "I tried to buy it last time I was here, but I didn't know there was a story behind it."

"Tell her, Clare," George said. "It's not like it's some dark secret or anything."

"Would you mind?" the woman asked. "I enjoy collecting, and every piece has its own little bit of history." She shrugged. "I guess that's one reason we refer to things as treasures."

"I suppose." Clare looked about to see if there might be someone in need of assistance.

"I'll handle things," George said, stepping out from behind the counter. "This is worth listening to," he said to the woman as he passed her on the way.

Clare took a large sheet of pink paper from under the counter and began wrapping one of the teacups. "About ten years ago … and almost to this month, actually … a frantic little black woman rushed into the store, carrying some kind of a package that appeared to have been hastily wrapped in newspaper…

Clare could see that the woman was highly agitated and moved quickly from behind the counter, fearful that she might knock over one of the display tables set with vintage glass wear. "Can I help you?" she asked. The woman appeared to be in early middle-age and neatly dressed.

"I need fifty dollars," the woman said, tearing at the newspaper. "That's all I need and I'll give you this."

"It's all right," Clare said, trying to calm the woman, who didn't appear at all like the homeless women who sometimes came soliciting at the shop. "Come to the counter and we'll take a look." Clare had always been modestly generous with the homeless so as not to make a target of herself. It wasn't easy to tell the grifters from the truly needy, but Clare gave all the same. In any case, this seemed different.

"I don't want anything more," the woman said, following. "Just fifty. That's all I need. You buy good things. And this here is good." She continued to pull desperately at the newspaper, dropping shreds onto the floor of the shop. Clare would deal with that later. Fortunately, the store wasn't busy at the moment.

Clare stepped behind the counter. "Let me help," she said, quietly, and reached across to take the package from the woman who shook her hands as if to hurry Clare along. After 20 years in the business of vintage collectibles, Clare was accustomed to items being brought into the store in every manner and condition. Some years earlier a man had shown up out front driving a fork lift that held an enormous eighteenth-century armoire clearly too large and cumbersome to fit through either the front door or the back.

As the woman shifted restlessly from one foot to the other, Clare used scissors to cut away the haphazard patches of scotch tape that secured the weighty object, whatever it was.

"Fifty is all I need," the woman repeated. "No more than that. No more."

When the last of the paper was dropped onto the floor behind the counter, Clare's eye's widened at the most remarkable Madonna and Child figurine she had ever seen. From the almost transparent purity of the glaze, she was sure at first glance that it was Meissen, but upon carefully turning it over, it did not have the familiar blue Meissen mark of crossed swords. Disappointing but definitely worth exploring.

The woman threw her hand out in front of Clare. "Fifty, please, and you keep it. Fifty and not a penny more is all I ask. But I do need it now."

Clare looked at the woman, fearful. Was she dealing with stolen property here? How did this woman gain possession of such a piece? Her desire to help the woman in any way she could had instantly turned to suspicion and caution. Besides, even as little as Clare could possibly know about the piece, she was certain that it was worth much more than fifty dollars. And what did the woman intend to do with the money, anyway? Was she on drugs? If she gave the woman money, would she herself be aiding and abetting some kind of crime?" She rubbed nervously at her neck. Of all the times for George to be at the post office. "Please," she said to the woman, at last. "I just can't give money for … for this. I need to know its origin … where it came from. How did you come by it? And I must ask if there isn't some other way that I can offer you help. Are you … sick? Are you afraid of something … or someone? I'd like to help." The woman appeared to be decently dressed and well groomed. What could her story be?

"Then help me with this. Please. This is mine. Right and legal." She lightly slapped her hand down on the top of the counter. "Right and legal. And I got no time. Fifty and I go and you keep it." As if as an afterthought, the woman rummaged through the pockets of her navy print jacket. "I'll find it. I'll find it," she kept repeating until she finally brought out a well-handled folded paper. "Here."

Clare opened and read it. "I, Ruby A. Breakmoor, sound of mind and body, leave to my loyal, long-time friend and servant woman, Carrie Mae Sparrow, my precious Meissen Madonna and Child, with the greatest of gratitude and respect." The paper bore what could have been an authentic signature, but how could Clare be sure. Ruby Breakmoor had been a prominent figure in Old Florida circles. Over the years, Clare had seen her a number of times riding past in her chauffeur-driven vintage Packard. How could she be sure this was indeed a true document. "I'm sorry to have to ask," Clare said in as kind a tone as possible, "could you please tell me your name?"

"My name?" The woman's voice had gone up an octave. "It's right there in front of you in the words of Miss Breakmoor herself – Carrie Mae Sparrow. The woman dug into her pockets again and pulled out a small black cloth purse, which she opened in order to produce a social security card and an outdated laminated ID, evidently the kind once used by employees of the Breakmoor estate. The ID bore the woman's photo, both documents bore the name Carrie Mae Sparrow.

"Miss…Sparrow, I am certain that this statue is worth much more … "

"I understand." The woman nodded. "I do. That's why fifty is all. Then nobody has any worries. No worries at all."

"May I please make a copy of these? It will take only a

minute," Clare said, still holding the woman's ID and the letter with Mrs. Broadmoor's name on it. "The printer is in the back room."

The woman had started pacing. "Hurry. Please. Hurry."

As Clare made her way to the back, it crossed her mind that she was leaving herself vulnerable. It wouldn't have been too difficult for the woman to get the register open or to make off with some expensive antique. But inexplicably, Clare wasn't worried. Careless or not, she stayed on task.

"Here you are," Clare said, counting fifty dollars in a mix of ten and five-dollar bills. "But I have an idea? Why don't you take the money and just keep the statue? I'm okay with that. I'm happy to help you out."

The woman pushed the money away. "Don't try giving me any handout. I want a fair trade. You understand? A fair trade."

Clare knew it was hopeless to do anything but just give her the money and she was glad to do it. "I want you to know, Miss Sparrow, that this statue remains your property and I will keep it for you. I will. It is not for sale, I promise."

But the woman was hardly listening, as she rolled up the bills and stuffed them into her small cloth purse, nodding. "You have been a blessing. A blessing." Then, she stopped still and looked directly into Clare's eyes. It was an earnest look, devoid of restlessness and anxiety. She put her hand on Clare's. "May you one day truly know the blessing you have been this day," she said, and out the door she went.

"What a fascinating story," the customer said, as she took her package. She rubbed her arm. "It gave me a chill. You never saw her again or heard anything about her?"

"Nothing," Martie chimed in. "All these years. Don't you think ten years is long enough to wait?"

"Did you ever determine the value of the piece?" the customer asked.

Clare hesitated. "I…well…one can never be sure about the value of obscure collectibles."

"That is so true," the customer said. "I've seen enough episodes of Antiques Roadshow where people are shocked to learn what their possessions are actually worth…sometimes precious, sometimes…well…fool's gold." She laughed then turned to leave. "And, I would have to agree, it probably is time to part with it. After all, why leave a few hundred dollars— if that's what you think it might be worth--sitting on a shelf. Better to put it in the bank, no? You can always give a bit of it to charity, if your conscience bothers you."

When the customer had left the store, Martie leaned closer to Clare and whispered. "I would have loved to see her expression if you had dared to tell her that its worth is in the neighborhood of forty-six thousand dollars. Our dear Mrs. Breakmoor had extravagant taste."

"Yes," Clare answered, wistful. She was remembering how curious a thing it had been when she first turned over the statue and found three unfamiliar initials instead of Meissen's signature crossed-swords, a great disappointment. It took some research, followed by verification from an antiquities expert, to discover that the signature on the bottom of the statue was from a Meissen period nearly one hundred and fifty years earlier. Likewise, Ruby Breakmoor's signature proved to be authentic. "A very generous woman—willing such a precious item to her loyal employee, Carrie Mae Sparrow. But then, it's nice when loyal employees who go above and beyond are treated in a way that is above and beyond." Using the small step-stool, Clare reached up and lifted the statue off the top shelf. She rarely took it down except to put it in the safe each evening. The detail and coloring were exquisite, subtle, ethereal. She ran her hand gently across the pale figures—The Virgin Mary holding the infant Jesus—then shook her head slowly. "I just can't sell it, Martie."

The following week, Clare attended the ribbon-cutting fundraiser for the new drug rehab clinic. She had decided at the last minute, although she couldn't imagine why because the store was a bit busy. She knew George and their part-timer, Steffie, could handle everything. But why on earth?

"See, I told you it would be a nice event," Martie said, after the gourmet luncheon that took place in an enormous white tent set with nearly twenty round tables of ten with white table cloths and opulent centerpieces of wildflowers set in crystal. An outer ring of long tables held dozens of items for the silent auction, everything from week-long vacations in the Bahamas to pairs of NBA season tickets.

Clare smiled in agreement. "I'm glad I came. Thanks,

Martie."

"What are good friends for? Not only that, but from everything I've heard, these folks have worked tirelessly to raise the necessary funds. A good cause, and long needed for sure."

Just prior to the tour of the state-of-the-art facility, the Master of Ceremonies, a local radio personality, introduced the Board of Directors and finally the Founder and Facility Director, Janella Greer. Amid the vibrant applause, the young woman stepped to the microphone.

"She's pretty," Martie said.

"Thank you all for coming out for this event and for your great generosity. This clinic is an idea, a place, a vision very much entrenched in my heart for more deeply personal reasons than you may realize. Let me begin by saying that we will need every penny of your ongoing support because there are so very many people out there who live the life I once lived.

"When I was sixteen, I was a drug addict. I dropped out of school. I stole money. Stole even from people I loved. I made life miserable not only for myself but for my family, a family that had adopted me to give me a better life. I took nearly everything from the one person who had given me the most, my adopted mother. A widow, no less. She had worked hard her whole life but the pension she received every month I spent on drugs. To make matters worse, she used up her savings trying to get me the help I needed. Even when I knew she had become desperate, I couldn't quit because I was desperate too. But one day, she packed a suitcase and took me to her brother's farm in Tennessee. A minister with a wonderful family. It saved my life and gave me a future. That was nearly ten years ago and my mother has since passed on, but to this day, I don't know where she got the money for that bus ticket…"

Clare and Martie turned and looked at each other, wide-eyed. "Do you suppose…?"

"Is it possible…?" was all Clare could say, as the young woman stepped to the front wall of the facility. She pulled the cord to remove the large purple satin cover from the dedication plaque, revealing the image of a face that for so many years had haunted Clare's memory.

"Ladies and Gentlemen, welcome to the Carrie Mae Sparrow Memorial Clinic."

Clare jumped to her feet, her hand over her mouth. Amid the uproar of applause, she recalled what Carrie Mae Sparrow had said to her that morning in the shop--"May you one day truly know the blessing you have been this day." Clare sat back down with Martie and calmly waited. Waited for the fanfare to finally subside. Waited for the crowd to finally disperse. That's when she would approach Janella Greer and tell her a story that came with a very special gift.

Here You Are, My Love

WELL, IT'S QUITE a time, isn't it, Steven? You can't see me, Dearest, and I still can't see you; there are so many people. Can't believe we're both here, and in this of all places. Who would have thought? I'm a nervous wreck. Your sister, Gwen, invited me. Can't imagine why I'm mentioning that—you probably know everything now—all of it. Who can say? The room is lovely, though, and very different from those banquet halls you spoke in all those years. Gwen did a beautiful job arranging things, I'll give her that.

I'm making my way in your direction. Fifteen years. I have such terrible flutters, and no idea how I'll handle the moment. It's such an elite group, and seeing you again…who knows what I'll feel. I'd rather be alone with you.

"Jean-Anne." It's Gwen. If she weren't such a snake, the warmth of her tone would almost seem sincere. "Jean-Anne." She's summoning. Summoning, mind you. Her diamond and sapphire earrings sparkle in the soft light of the crystal chandeliers—the shine of hard stone, like her smile. The more glitter the better, I suppose, for the richest woman in the room. I won't acknowledge her. You are the most important one here, and I will never forgive her.

I hope you don't mind this Ann Taylor suit I'm wearing—dark isn't it, but it helps me blend in as if I were just another piece of hay in the bale, so conveniently unnoticed. It was a problem back then, Darling—being unnoticed, I mean. Gwen said you needed a partner much more adept at the social arts. Yes, that's actually the term she used.

I know you would have preferred me in something softer, a flowing dress, as you called it.

"I have a mind to twirl you," you once said. I had to laugh, it seemed so unlike you, but you did exactly that, I'll never forget—our Vermont getaway, Christmas week, a lifetime ago. We stayed through New Year's, and we turned round the dance floor to the last song they played before the countdown to midnight. You caught me in your arms and held me. I nearly cried seeing you so free and joyful. Auld Lang Syne. Gwen was livid when we got back to Boston.

"Steven!" I remember how she blew out her words like shrapnel. "Do you really think your reputation can afford this kind of frivolity?" She hated the way you made light of it. It must have frightened her to believe she was seeing you self-destruct. How sad. Sad for us, as it turned out.

I'm passing among the murmuring clusters of your admirers, trying not to make eye contact with anyone, although I doubt there's a person here who knows who I am. There was some talk back then—you knew but didn't care. Anyway, that ended long ago, as we did, with quiescent finality. Gwen saw to it; all part of the plan to get me out of your life. Did you know? Of course not. You were never to learn the truth behind my leaving—you would never have stood for it. She knew that.

Gwen made a good case for me to go, Steven, and I swear I fought it at first, but I was coerced by her wicked logic. She said I would only hinder your chances for tenure and research funding, and all the rest—everything you were destined to achieve. She had the insolence to offer me money.

"You are clearly a decent woman," she had granted, "and highly intelligent, no doubt." How generous of her—imagine. "Fine attributes that may serve you well, Jean-Anne. But you would need much more than that to help my brother. This is a different world from what you are accustomed to."

I was simply not…how did she put it…the right fit—a mere distraction who lacked the clout within this privileged and scholarly community to help you accomplish your objectives… excuse me, Dearest, *her* objectives.

And, yes, yes, I knew it would break your heart the way it would break mine. Forgive me, Steven. But I also knew your sense of duty would call you back to the work you were so brilliantly cut out for. You had so much to offer the world— how could I dare risk your future. You do see that it worked, don't you? This room—the accolades, the reverence with which they regard you. They are here to pay tribute. I'm so very proud of you, Darling.

How I long to be alone with you. Silly, isn't it, to want to make an accounting of myself, like a schoolgirl who stayed out too late, as if I haven't spoken to you in my dreams through all the lonely years. What do they know of you anyway, this mob of pompous intellects who have their own secrets? What do they know of your depth, beyond all intellectual capacity? They share their stories of you to let their egos rub elbows with your greatness. Oh, Darling, I'm too harsh, I know. I know. You have friends here. Forgive me. As you would imagine, I'm just not myself right now.

I saw you in Scientific American and searched *Dr. Steven Sandgaard* on line to follow your achievements. Truthfully, I also wanted to see if there was any word that you had married. I watched you on CSpan once and looked closely for a wedding ring. You didn't have one. Believe me, Dearest, there was only the most fleeting consolation in that. I haven't a ring either.

I was shocked when Gwen called. "Please come," she said, her voice dripping with sentiment. "It's only right, after all." After all? After all the venom she spewed when you and I were together. But you were steadfast in your love for me. I have never forgotten. Never.

The music is lovely. I wish it were Mozart instead of Brahms—he's so cheerless. I loved going to the Symphony with you. Respighi's Pines of Rome, your favorite, became my favorite too. But we did love Dvorzak, didn't we? We went for cappuccino after the…oh, stop, stop. For God's sake, why am I going on like this? What am I thinking? My mind is in a frenzy,

Steven. My heart is beating in my ears. I should turn and go. I could slip out exactly as I slipped in. You would forgive me; I know you would. I love you so. That will never change. I'm not prepared for this.

There are people around you, but I can see you more clearly now. I feel a catch in my throat as I draw near. I remember you in your tweeds, unassuming, half-distracted, sweet. But I must say the fine navy does suit you. Did Gwen select your clothes? No matter. The tie is that perfect blue, the way I remember your eyes. I feel a bit overcome by the cloying fragrance of the flowers.

You look…there's that catch again…you look, quite nearly yourself, only much thinner now, considering your recent illness, which I knew nothing about, Darling, or I would have come, no matter what, I would have come. I'm past wondering why Gwen didn't call sooner. She must have felt around for a bit of compassion in that icy cavern of a heart and come up empty.

I had hoped I wouldn't cry, but here you are, my love, in your fine titanium box. I kneel here now and wonder: is it very much like the box in which you lived your life? The bronze torchieres at either end stand like sentinels, guarding you still. Your eyes are so tightly shut. So tightly shut. My God, it is true, isn't it? It's true.

Oh, Steven. Steven. What is there for us now? I am twirling again. My pain is turning in on itself, grinding so deep within me that it will never be lifted or removed. I wish I could kiss you awake, unfold your hands and lead you off your tufted satin pillow. I wish I could take you back to what might have been, but in truth, my darling…in truth…all I have left to wish for is to lie beside you, my broken heart pressed against your lifeless arm, and hold you through all eternity.

The Christmas Samaritan

THE ICY PAVEMENT crunched under foot as Vanessa trudged across the mall parking lot toward her silver Volvo. She carried three large shopping bags that banged clumsily against her legs with every step—gifts for her local Angel Tree toy drive. Once again, she had vowed to remember the true meaning of the season.

Vanessa had reminded her husband and daughters—no more designer handbags, no more extravagant spa packages. "Let's keep things simple, and focus on those in real need."

"Sure, Mom," the girls had said.

"You bet," said Jeff, and kissed her on the cheek.

They all knew that her track record for good deeds wasn't very good—like the time she offered to string Christmas lights on the bushes outside their elderly neighbors' home. The wires somehow shorted, causing a flare that burned the couple's juniper hedge to the ground.

She set the shopping bags in the trunk of the Volvo, then moved out into the clogged lanes of holiday traffic. The car heater soon warmed up, heightening the aroma of her evergreen car scent.

When she reached Warren Street, she turned north toward home. "At last," she said with a happy sigh. The traffic would be lighter now. She put in another Christmas CD and sang along with The Mormon Tabernacle Choir at the top of her lungs. She almost wished it were nighttime so she could enjoy the festive array of lights that traced the houses and dotted the trees like moon drops.

Vanessa thought about the toys she'd purchased—dolls and teddy bears and little plastic tea sets, action heroes and bright yellow Tonka trucks. She delighted in the thoughts of the boys and girls who would open them on Christmas morning, and hoped there would not be another choking hazard recall like the year before.

About a mile up the road, she saw St. Ann's Episcopal Church with its large colorful sign in the parking lot, "Toy Drive Drop-Off." An SUV was parked there, its back door standing open. She smiled as she went past, thinking of others who might be dropping off toys and clothing. What a glorious season, she thought—people caring for people. She couldn't wait to wrap all the toys she'd purchased.

Farther along, Vanessa noticed a woman walking on the sidewalk, struggling against the wind. She was headed in the direction of the bus stop half a block away, weighed down by shopping bags. This was definitely someone who needed help. Vanessa slowed the car alongside the curb and rolled down the passenger window.

"Excuse me," she called to the woman.

The woman, bundled up in an insulated coat, wore a scarf, ninja-like, across the bottom half of her face. She didn't look up.

"Excuse me. Hello," Vanessa called out again. She knew it must be hard for the woman to hear her. "May I give you a lift? It's awfully cold."

The woman turned slowly, then glanced behind her.

"It's okay." Vanessa sensed the woman's caution. "It's safe. I'm just a lady like you, out Christmas shopping. I'd be happy to give you a ride. Just put your things in the back seat."

The woman did as Vanessa said and got in beside her, bringing a rush of arctic air.

"You must be freezing, and who knows how long you'd have waited for the bus."

The woman loosened the scarf a little and in a low voice said, "Thank you."

Vanessa drove off. "Where can I take you?"

"Do you know where Clean Load is?"

"Clean…?"

"Clean Load," the woman repeated, a little louder. She pointed ahead. "The laundromat. It's in that Walmart shopping center. Up a ways."

"Oh, okay, sure. I know where that is. But I'd be happy to drive you home."

"It's okay. My husband will come get me. He'll be waiting

for me to call."

"I'm Vanessa."

The woman nodded.

"It looks like you've done a bit of shopping too." Vanessa said. "I just came from the mall. It's crazy there."

"Mm," said the woman.

"Do you have a big family?"

"So-so," said the woman.

They continued in silence. Vanessa let the cheerful holiday music fill the void, realizing that sometimes people who get a helping hand feel embarrassed by their predicament. Whether this woman spoke to her or not, Vanessa knew she appreciated the ride. This was exactly the kind of thing Vanessa loved doing, even if there was that time when an elderly woman she offered a ride to screamed at her and broke her back window with a rock. This poor woman may not even thank her, but it didn't matter—virtue is its own reward.

At that moment, of course, Vanessa had no way of knowing that very shortly an all-points-bulletin would be issued for a silver Volvo, observed as the getaway car in the theft of hundreds of dollars in merchandise from the toy drop-off at St. Ann's Episcopal Church on Warren Street. The Clean Load Laundromat parking lot would become a very busy place when three police cars, red and blue lights flashing crazily, dashed in to surround Vanessa and her passenger.

Later on, after making her one phone call from the police station, it would occur to Vanessa that there were a lot of things you might expect someone to say to you when you tried helping a person in need. "Step out with your hands in the air," was not one of them.

Wishbones

ON MY NINTH birthday, I sat before a marshmallow cream cake, eyes squeezed shut, and with the heat of ten candles—one for good measure, my mother always said—warming the tip of my nose, I made my wish. It was different from the wish I had made at Thanksgiving when I won that coveted piece of turkey carcass in the annual wishbone split. Different from the one I had made the year before with my tooth under my pillow.

My wishes were always different. I had wished to be a princess. I had wished for a pet monkey and a BB gun. I had wished that Bartholomew Ponte, who sat next to me in Sister Ann Stephanie's music class, would fall in love with me so we could get married when we grew up.

Technically, you could make a wish any time, but you had to work for the big ones. You had to blow out all the candles at once, you had to lose a tooth, you had to be better at cracking that wishbone than your cousin Anthony.

"Anthony has grown a lot," my Uncle Frank had cautioned one Thanksgiving. "He's a big boy now. I think he means business."

But Anthony didn't have the right thumb action—there's this leverage thing my father had taught me, like getting your wrist over in an arm-wrestling match. As it turned out, it really didn't matter. All the thumb-overs and lost teeth and candle-blowing didn't make a single wish come true. Not one. That Christmas when I had wished for a floor-length satin cape covered in sequins, I got a bathrobe.

Once, I wished that Sister Rose Raphael would grow a wart on her nose the size of a gumball. I ended up feeling relieved when that one didn't come true. Sister had been right, after all—I should not have tied Steven Sawicki's shoelaces together while he was reading *Evangeline* to the class.

The year I turned eight, I had figured out a way to trick the system. I wished that any one thing I would wish for during the whole entire year ahead would come true, anything at all. Just one. That my hair would never be frizzy again. That my teeth would straighten up without the braces. That we would have ten snow days in a row with no school. That I would get an "A" in math. On and on. Clever as I thought I was, not one wish came true.

It didn't help that nobody gave you odds on this stuff the way they do with Powerball—*your chance of having your wishbone wish come true is one in seven hundred and fifty-five million.* Maybe then I would have had a clue. But maybe not. People don't seem to care about the odds.

"What did you wish for, Honey?" my Aunt Rita had

whispered to me, then quickly recanted, holding the side of her head as if in pain. "Ooooh, don't tell me. Don't tell me. I wouldn't want to be the one to jinx you. Tell me what it is when it comes true."

Turns out, I had nothing to tell.

I decided to talk to my Aunt Katie about this. Aunt Katie was an interesting person. She was tall and pretty and wore bright red lipstick and the kind of clothes you saw in magazines, clothes I wanted to wear when I got older. She told whacky stories that surprised people and made them laugh. Things happened to Aunt Katie that didn't happen to other people, like the time a man's umbrella accidentally hooked the handle of her purse while she was standing on a crowded subway platform and yanked her onto the wrong train. The man with the umbrella later became my Uncle Bill.

Or the time she jumped behind the wheel of a crowded uptown bus when the driver fainted. She somehow managed to hold the driver's head back with her elbow, grab the wheel and press the ball of her brown leather sling-back shoe hard enough against the brake to stop the lumbering vehicle, but not before bumping up the first three steps of The Metropolitan Museum of Art. It made all the papers. She was a hero.

"Aunt Katie, can I ask you a question about wishing?" It was the end of another Thanksgiving Day, and she and Uncle Bill were ready to go home. She was in my parents' bedroom sitting in front of the mirror putting on lipstick.

"Wishing?" She squeezed the word out through pursed lips

that she traced with flame red strokes.

"Wishing," I said.

"Wishing for what?"

"Just wishing," I stood behind her, communicating through the mirror. "Did you ever make a wish?"

Her eyes grew large with surprise. So much of her was in her eyes. "Did I ever make a wish? Are you kidding? Absolutely. We were born to wish."

"Did any of your wishes ever come true?"

She put her finger to her chin. "Let me think--can't come up with anything at the moment."

That was Aunt Katie—never took much time to ponder things. I really liked that about her. She was what they called spontaneous. It aggravated my mother, who was always telling me to think.

"Well, then, what's the good of it?" I said to Aunt Katie. I needed to get somewhere with this. I had no intention of wasting any more teeth, wind or wishbones.

The apartment where we lived was one flight up, and Uncle Bill was already downstairs by the front door. "Kate," he yelled, "if you don't hurry, we'll miss the last express train." Uncle Bill was what my Dad called "a solid guy," the kind of guy you could always depend on and trust. And anyone could tell he was crazy about Aunt Katie. "Kate," he yelled up again.

Aunt Katie looked astonished. "What's the good of it? What's the good of making a wish?" She turned and called to my mother in the kitchen. "What are you teaching this child?"

I hated the word child. What was I, two?

My mother was a smart and serious person who enjoyed intelligent frivolity but had a very low tolerance for silliness or slapstick. She couldn't stand Milton Berle; she loved Victor Borge. "Bill is calling you," my mother hollered back.

"But if you can't even remember if one of your wishes came true," I said, "then maybe they never did."

"But they must have," Aunt Katie said, tugging her black fur hat into place. "I have everything I want. I must have wished for at least some of them. What more could I possibly have wished for?"

"But none of my wishes or dreams ever come true."

"Oh, now wait a minute." She folded her arms with the authority of a teacher who had just caught you at something. "Are we talking about wishing…or dreaming?"

"Kate!" Uncle Bill never sounded more than just a little impatient when it came to Aunt Kate. Everyone knew he adored her.

"They're the same thing, aren't they?" I asked. I knew it wasn't nice for either one of us to ignore Uncle Bill, but this had to be more important than the last express train.

"Oh, no. No." Aunt Katie was adamant. She stood and yanked at the belt of her coat to tighten it. Even all covered up in a heavy woolen winter coat, she reminded me of a movie star. "Wishing and dreaming are two entirely different things. It's important for people to know that. A dream is something you work towards and help make come true. You dream about becoming a writer, so you read a lot and go to school to study literature. Then you write a lot. And one day you could become a writer. A journalist maybe." She shrugged. "I dreamed about becoming a fashion designer, but I never did anything about it. In any case, a wish is different. Oh, yes, very different. A wish is meant to be something so big and outrageous that you can't accomplish it on your own, so that if it comes true it's as if… as if…a miracle happened." She spread her arms expansively, then brought her hands together over her heart and nodded. "It's that different."

I had to stop and consider this. I told her about how I had wished for a pet monkey.

Aunt Katie put her hand on my shoulder and looked me in the eye. "You know, Margaret, I did not say that all wishes are good wishes. They are not. And some wishes don't come true just for our own good. Only movie monkeys are cute. The rest are really very dirty and when they get older they rip your eye out."

I told her about Bartholomew Ponte and how I had also wished to become a princess.

"Well, Margaret, it just may be that it's not time yet to pick a person to marry. You're only nine. You might end up meeting someone you'll like better. And what about this?" She brought her face very close to mine, and whispered. "What if Bartholomew Ponte grows up to be crazy?"

That was certainly a possibility I had never considered. There was this man in the neighborhood who always walked around talking to himself and waving a string on the end of a stick. I remembered wondering what he must have been like as a boy. Now I was thinking if possibly he was just like Bartholomew Ponte. "Okay, then what about a princess?" I asked. "A princess is a good thing, isn't it?" Surely, I had gotten something right.

Aunt Katie straightened herself and took a deep breath. "See…it's like this. It's okay to watch movies, but we really shouldn't take them too seriously. For example, a princess is watched over at all times. They read her diary. She can't eat hotdogs, or ride the Cyclone at Coney Island. And if they allow her to have ice cream, she can only eat vanilla. A princess would never be allowed to eat toasted coconut."

"Are you sure about that?"

"Cross my heart," she said, with a noble nod.

I confessed to her about Sister Rose Raphael's wart.

Aunt Katie narrowed her eyes. "We must never wish bad things on others, Margaret. Right there, that could negate all your other wishes."

I didn't know what negate meant, but I got the picture.

I heard stomping in the hall. Uncle Bill!

Aunt Katie, still unfazed, took me by the shoulders and leaned in close to my face. I had once wished for long, pretty eyelashes just like hers. "We were all born to wish, Margaret. We have no idea how it really works, but we do it because it delights the heart and gives us hope, which feeds our soul… like praying…even though the truth is that most times…"

Uncle Bill came through the door, the cold air still hanging on him, and took Aunt Katie by the arm. "Catherine Gallagher," he said, even now with a measure of graciousness, "how many times do I have to call you? You do this all the time. It's freezing out." I heard him laugh as they went out.

My heart sank. "Most times what?" I followed them to the front door.

"Most times…" Aunt Katie was breathless hurrying after Uncle Bill in her shiny black high heels that clacked on the wooden floor where the carpet ended. "…it's all just a big poof."

My father stood there smiling with the newspaper in one hand and his glasses on the tip of his nose. As Aunt Katie and Uncle Bill flew past, he gave them a cheerful goodbye and closed the door quietly behind them, shaking his head.

"A big poof?" I thought.

My mother was in the kitchen surrounded by crusted pans, half-empty china platters, and a giant picked-over bird.

"Ma," I said, plucking one last bit of marshmallow off the leftover sweet potatoes, "how do you feel about making wishes?"

"What are you talking about?" she asked, scraping off the plates. My aunts had always volunteered to help do this, but my mother politely refused, understanding that while they were chattering away, distracted, some of the Reed and Barton was going out with the scraps.

"I mean when you make a wish, what do you think happens?"

She looked up at me. "Is this another one of Uncle Frank's tricky puzzle questions…like where do they bury the survivors?"

"No, I mean I was talking to Aunt Katie about wishing, and…"

"My sister," she said, carrying a stack of dishes to the sink. "I love her, but…you know, Margaret…I always tell you…she's scattery. She sees messages on her raisin toast."

"Aunt Katie says we were born to wish."

My mother rinsed a plate under the steaming water. "We were born to behave ourselves, do what we're supposed to, and not annoy people with silly ideas."

"Uncle Bill pulled her away before we could really finish."

"Uncle Bill," she said, nodding. "Now there's a man who will have no trouble getting into heaven. You should wish to marry a man as kind and patient as your Uncle Bill."

"But, Ma, that's the problem." I was almost pleading now. "There's no point wishing for anything. Nothing ever comes true."

"Well, here's a wish—I wish you would comb your hair once in a while." She moved more dishes around. "Have you done any reading since you've been off from school?"

"Can we call Aunt Katie tomorrow?"

"Your father would have a fit," she said, handing me a dishtowel, "calling like that for no good reason. How about wishing that money grows on trees?"

That night I tried to figure it all out. I lay in bed for over an hour, then quietly got up, went to the closet, and took the White Owl cigar box containing my old wishbone treasures off the shelf. One was wrapped in multi-colored thread. One was covered in bright pink glitter. That was the year I wished to become a champion ice skater. One was wrapped in thin leather strips from the year I wished to be a rodeo cowgirl, racing around the barrels at Madison Square Garden. I stared at them for a while, put away the box, and went back to bed.

A month later, as we sat down to Christmas dinner, I whispered to Aunt Katie, "What did you mean by 'poof'?"

She had no idea what I was talking about. I reminded her.

"Ahh, yes. Well, it's like your mother said—she *wishes* I wouldn't fill your head with things. See? It's not really a true wish; it's just a poof!"

"I'll give *you* a poof." My mother said. She set the bowl of mashed potatoes on the table. "Who's saying grace?"

My birthday was coming up in March. There would be more candle-blowing and more wishes. I needed to talk to Aunt Katie again, but the poker game was under way and she was winning. There was no getting her away from the table. New Year's Eve they all went dancing. Aunt Katie loved to dance. She and Uncle Bill were the best at it. I had seen them dance at all the weddings, the way he held her close and slow turned her, smiling the whole time. I wanted to do that with the man I would marry. Now, however, New Year's Eve had come and gone and I knew I wouldn't see Aunt Katie again until Easter. But in between, a terrible thing happened—poor

Uncle Bill died in his sleep.

I felt bad for Aunt Katie, all dressed in black, standing in front of the casket. I wasn't even supposed to be there. My fifteen-year-old cousin, Franny, was babysitting me and thought of it as kind of an adventure to go to the funeral parlor. Neither one of us had ever been to one. I had often peeked in the door of Falcone's Funeral Home on the avenue, but only saw a lot of flowers and people in black. No bodies.

My mother was furious. She had caught sight of us as soon as we came in the front door. "How could you even think of coming here," she said, taking Franny by the arm and pulling her aside. She gestured to the room where the casket was. "I don't want her going in there." She turned to me. "You sit right here. Go in the bathroom and comb your hair."

A few minutes later, Aunt Katie came into the Ladies Room. I had never seen her face so plain and puffy. It was streaked with tears. She looked like she could be her own twin—the one who wouldn't ever care to dance or laugh much. But she was still beautiful to me. It was just the two of us and I couldn't think of anything to say except "I'm sorry, Aunt Katie," and gave her a hug. Her dress felt soft against my face and had the smell of lilacs. I remember thinking how wonderful it was that beauty could exist right along with terrible sadness.

She held me close for a long moment, then she wet a paper towel and pressed it against her eyes. I stood watching her in the mirror and thought of the day I was walking along the sidewalk outside church and saw a butterfly someone had stepped on.

Aunt Katie blew her nose. "You know what I wish, Margaret?"

She sounded like someone with a very bad cold. I shook my head.

"I wish I had been on time, so Uncle Bill didn't always have to wait for me in the freezing cold. I wish I had been more thoughtful and let him win at cards. Just once I should have let him win. I wish I had made his life easy." She smiled at me, as a tiny ball of water rolled down her pale cheek, traced the outline of her un-powdered nose, and rested at the edge of her mouth.

That night, when I was unable to sleep, I went to the closet and took my White Owl cigar box off the shelf.

"We were born to wish," Aunt Katie had said.

I removed the wishbone with the multi-colored thread and placed it on the dresser. The next day, I went to the little mahogany cabinet next to my mother's favorite chair and opened her crochet drawer. I found the brightest red silk thread I could and re-wrapped that wishbone. I used black silk thread to cover the tip, in memory of Uncle Bill. I wrapped it tight, closed my eyes, and pressed it against my heart. I would wish the best of all things for everyone I loved. And I would never stop.

About the Author

MARY FLYNN IS an award-winning author of poetry, fiction and nonfiction. Her writing is an imaginative mix of humor, pathos and irony that explores the human experience, often with a surprising twist. She is also an expert on leadership and service delivery, having taught and spoken for Disney Institute for nearly fifteen years before three-quarters of a million professionals including CEOs of major corporations.

As a full-time staff writer for Hallmark Cards in Kansas City, Mary wrote for every category of Hallmark greetings as well as Hallmark's special poetry collections. Since then, Mary's observational humor has appeared in the *Sunday New York Times*, Newsday and other dailies and magazines. She was a poetry prizewinner in the *Writer's Digest* Writing Competition, a double finalist in the Royal Palm Literary Awards, and her short story, "Jeremiah's Orchard," is published in *The Saturday Evening Post Anthology of Great American Fiction*.

Mary recently retired from her international speaking role with Disney to write full-time.

She continues to inspire organizational change and inform professional development with her groundbreaking program, "The Million Dollar Question."

On the lighter side, "Confessions of a Hallmark Greeting Card Writer" is Mary's fun opportunity to present an engaging program that delights her audiences with the how-to as well as the mishaps behind the scene at Hallmark. Her debut novel, *Margaret Ferry*, which has a five-star rating on Amazon, won the Gold Medal in fiction, the Silver Medal in Religious writing and the Silver Medal in Christian writing. Her Silver award-winner, *"Disney's Secret Sauce—the-little-known factor behind the business world's most legendary leadership,"* is enjoying five stars on Amazon.

To find out more about
Mary's books and talks please visit »

WWW.MARYFLYNNWRITES.COM

www.ingramcontent.com/pod-product-compliance
Lightning Source LLC
Chambersburg PA
CBHW070658100726
47907CB00007B/2259

9 781732 838048